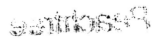

NICK the SIDEKICK

Peachtree

DAVE WHAMOND

KIDS CAN PRESS

To my budding superheroes, Maria and Zac, and my wife, Carla, aka Wonder Woman.

Kids Can Press gratefully acknowledges the financial support of the Government of Ontario, through the Ontario Media Development Corporation; the Ontario Arts Council; the Canada Council for the Arts; and the Government of Canada, through the CBF, for our publishing activity.

Published in Canada and the U.S. by Kids Can Press Ltd.
25 Dockside Drive, Toronto, ON M5A 0B5

Kids Can Press is a Corus Entertainment Inc. company

www.kidscanpress.com

The artwork in this book was rendered in pen and ink and digital watercolor.
The text is set in Boudoir and Blambot FXPro.

Edited by Jennifer Stokes
Designed by Michael Reis

Printed and bound in Shenzhen, China, in 9/2017 by C & C Offset

CM 18 0 9 8 7 6 5 4 3 2 1

Library and Archives Canada Cataloguing in Publication

Whamond, Dave, author, illustrator

     Nick the sidekick / written and illustrated by Dave Whamond.

ISBN 978-1-77138-355-4 (hardcover)

     1. Graphic novels. I. Title.

PN6733.W43N53 2018   j741.5'971   C2017-903195-3

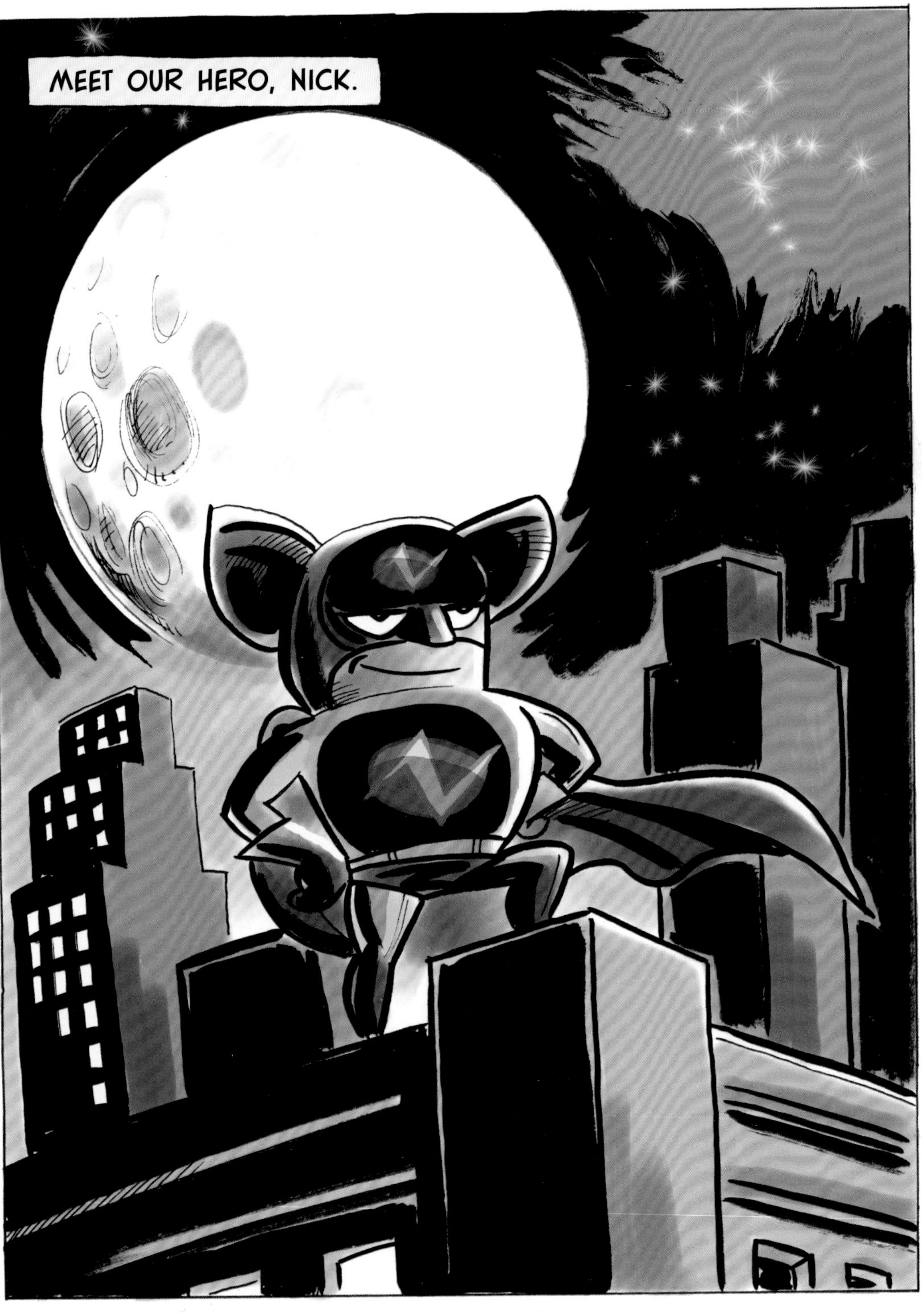
MEET OUR HERO, NICK.

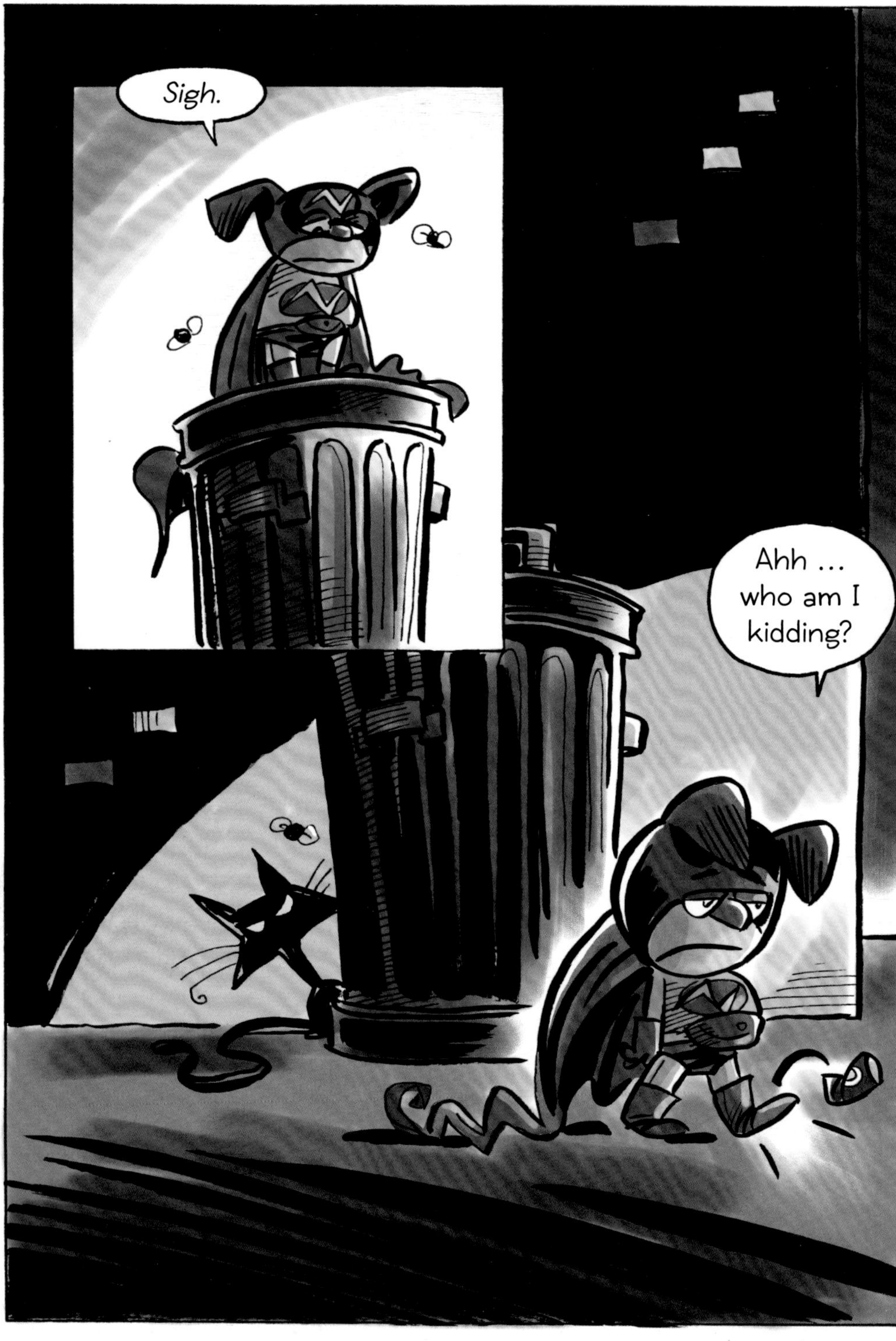
Sigh.
Ahh ... who am I kidding?

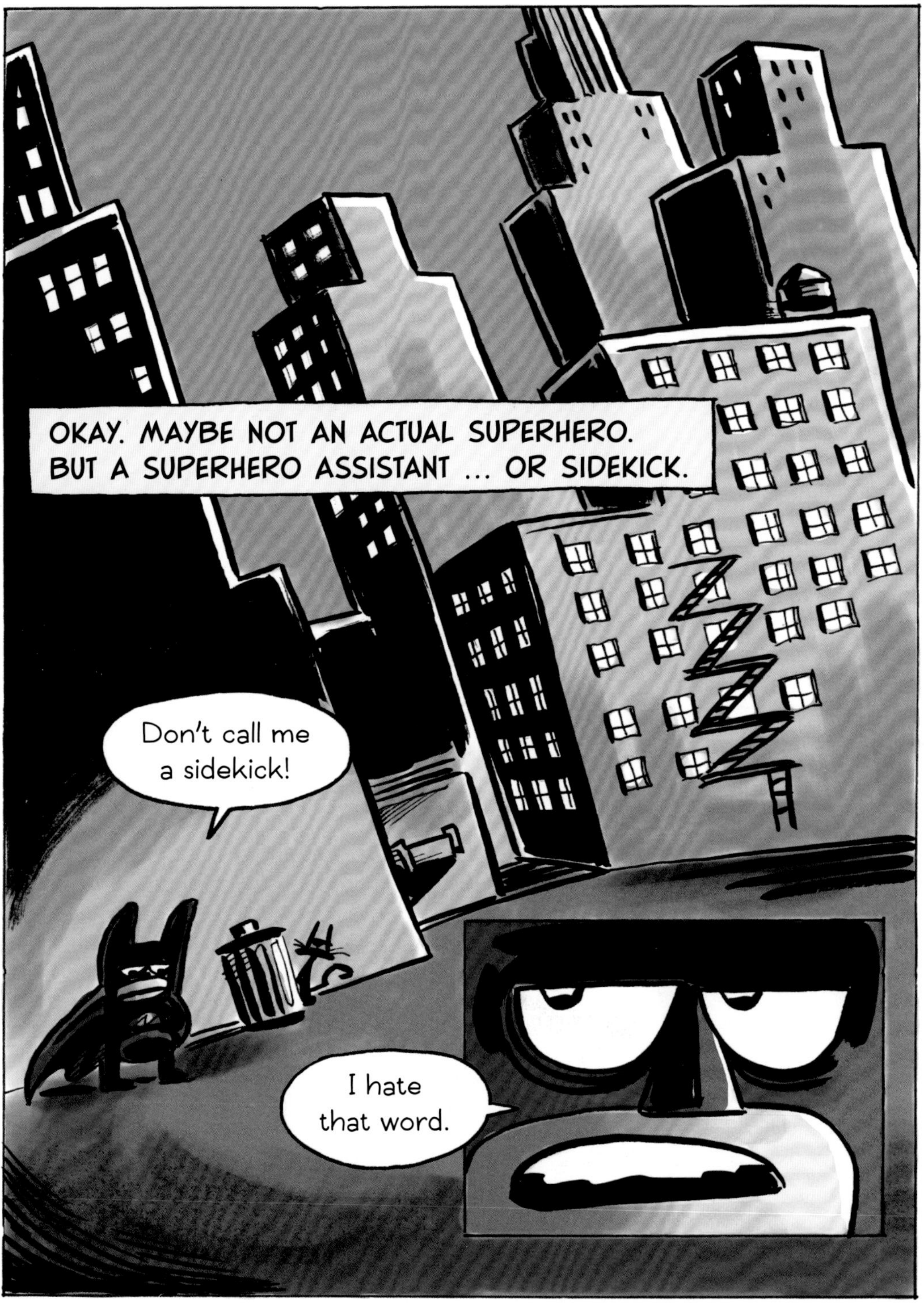
OKAY. MAYBE NOT AN ACTUAL SUPERHERO. BUT A SUPERHERO ASSISTANT ... OR SIDEKICK.
Don't call me a sidekick!
I hate that word.

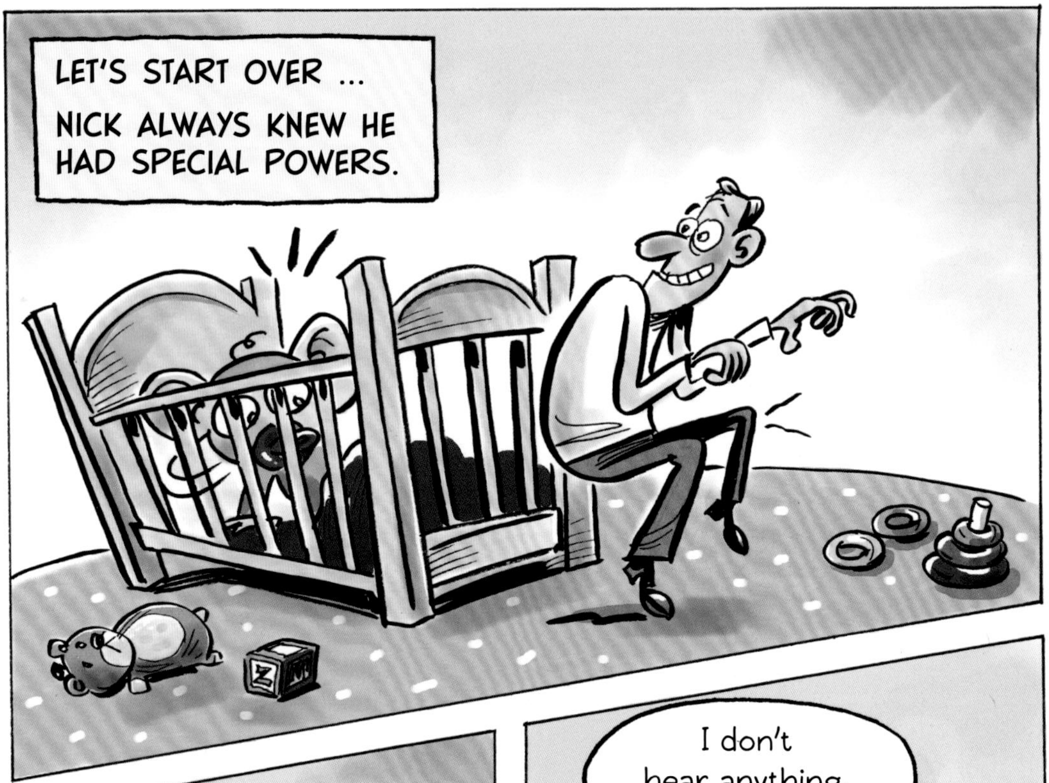
LET'S START OVER ...
NICK ALWAYS KNEW HE HAD SPECIAL POWERS.

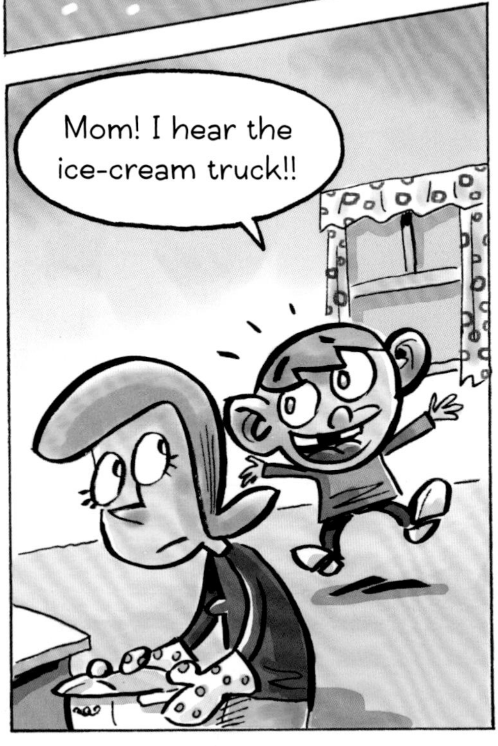
Mom! I hear the ice-cream truck!!

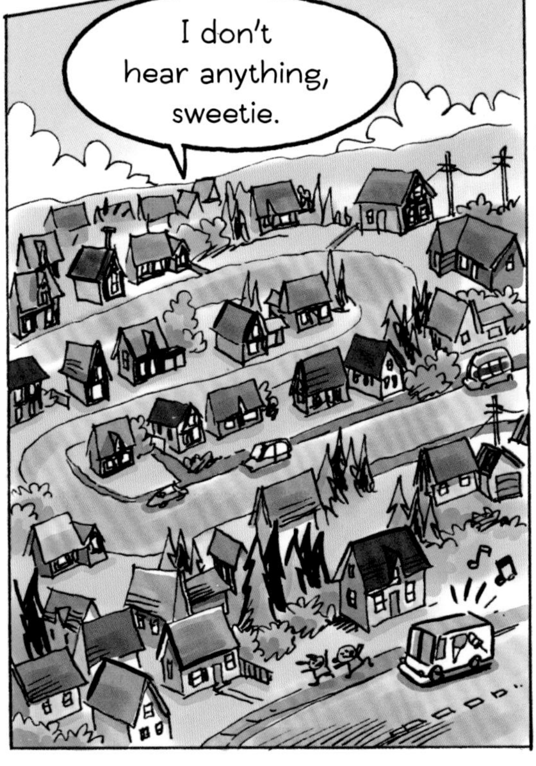
I don't hear anything, sweetie.

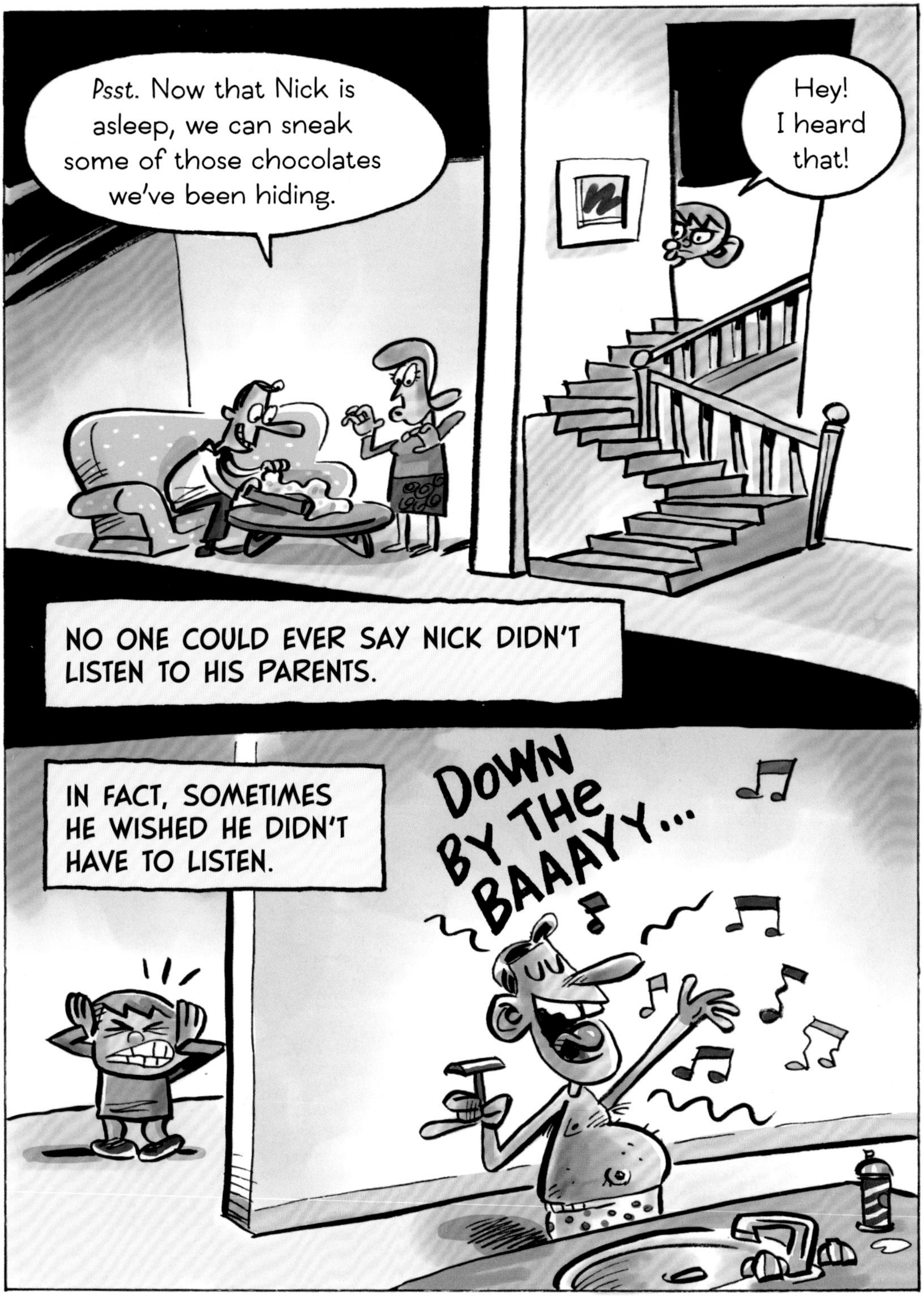

Psst. Now that Nick is asleep, we can sneak some of those chocolates we've been hiding.
Hey! I heard that!
NO ONE COULD EVER SAY NICK DIDN'T LISTEN TO HIS PARENTS.
IN FACT, SOMETIMES HE WISHED HE DIDN'T HAVE TO LISTEN.
DOWN BY THE BAAAYY...

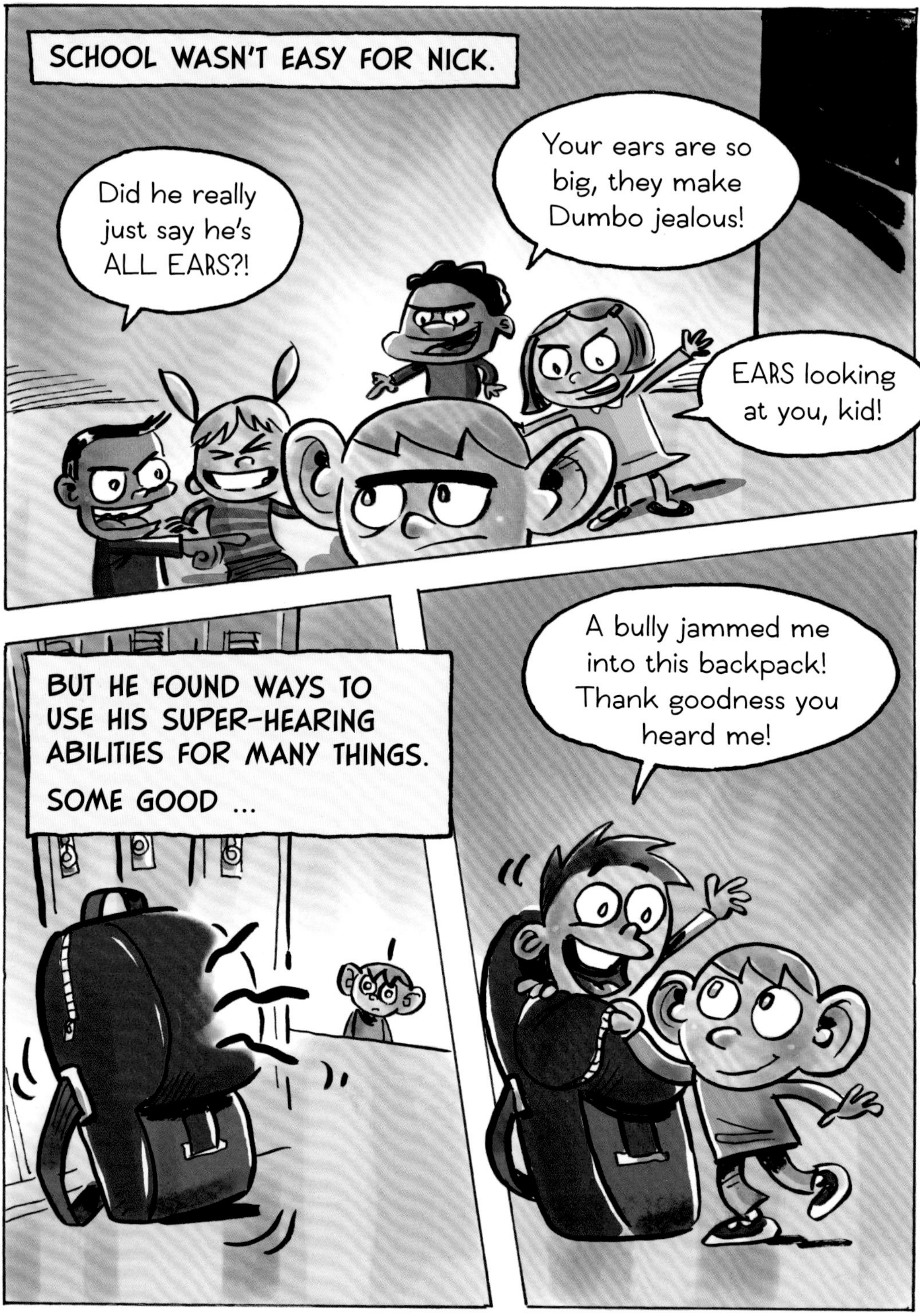
SCHOOL WASN'T EASY FOR NICK.
Did he really just say he's ALL EARS?!
Your ears are so big, they make Dumbo jealous!
EARS looking at you, kid!
BUT HE FOUND WAYS TO USE HIS SUPER-HEARING ABILITIES FOR MANY THINGS.
SOME GOOD ...
A bully jammed me into this backpack! Thank goodness you heard me!

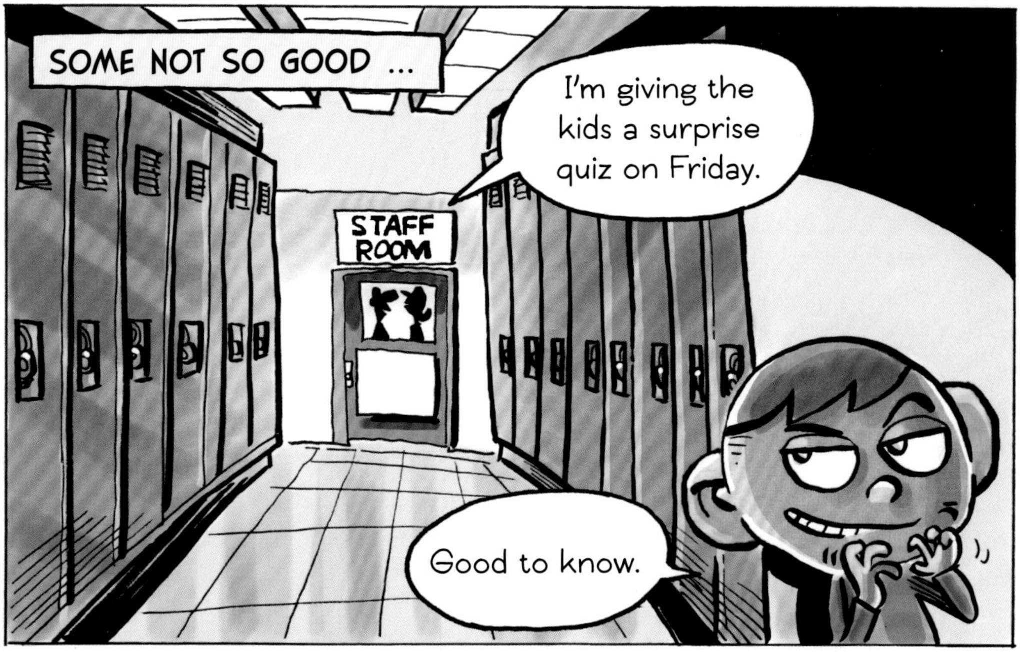
SOME NOT SO GOOD ...
I'm giving the kids a surprise quiz on Friday.
STAFF ROOM
Good to know.

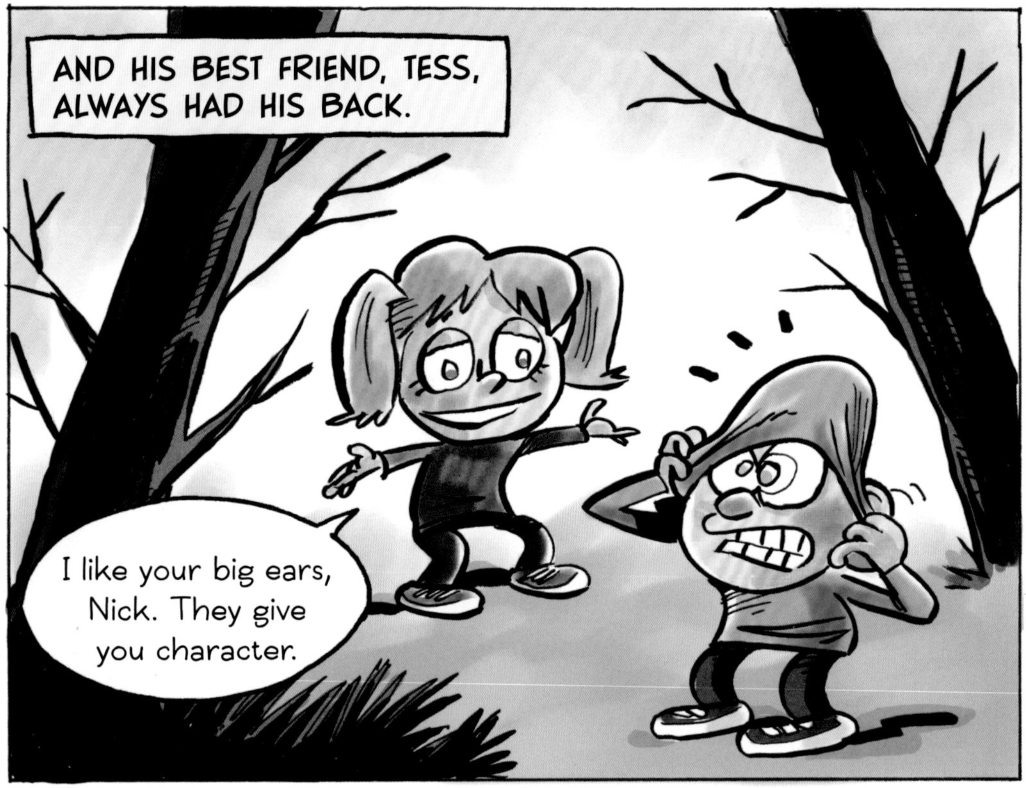
AND HIS BEST FRIEND, TESS, ALWAYS HAD HIS BACK.
I like your big ears, Nick. They give you character.

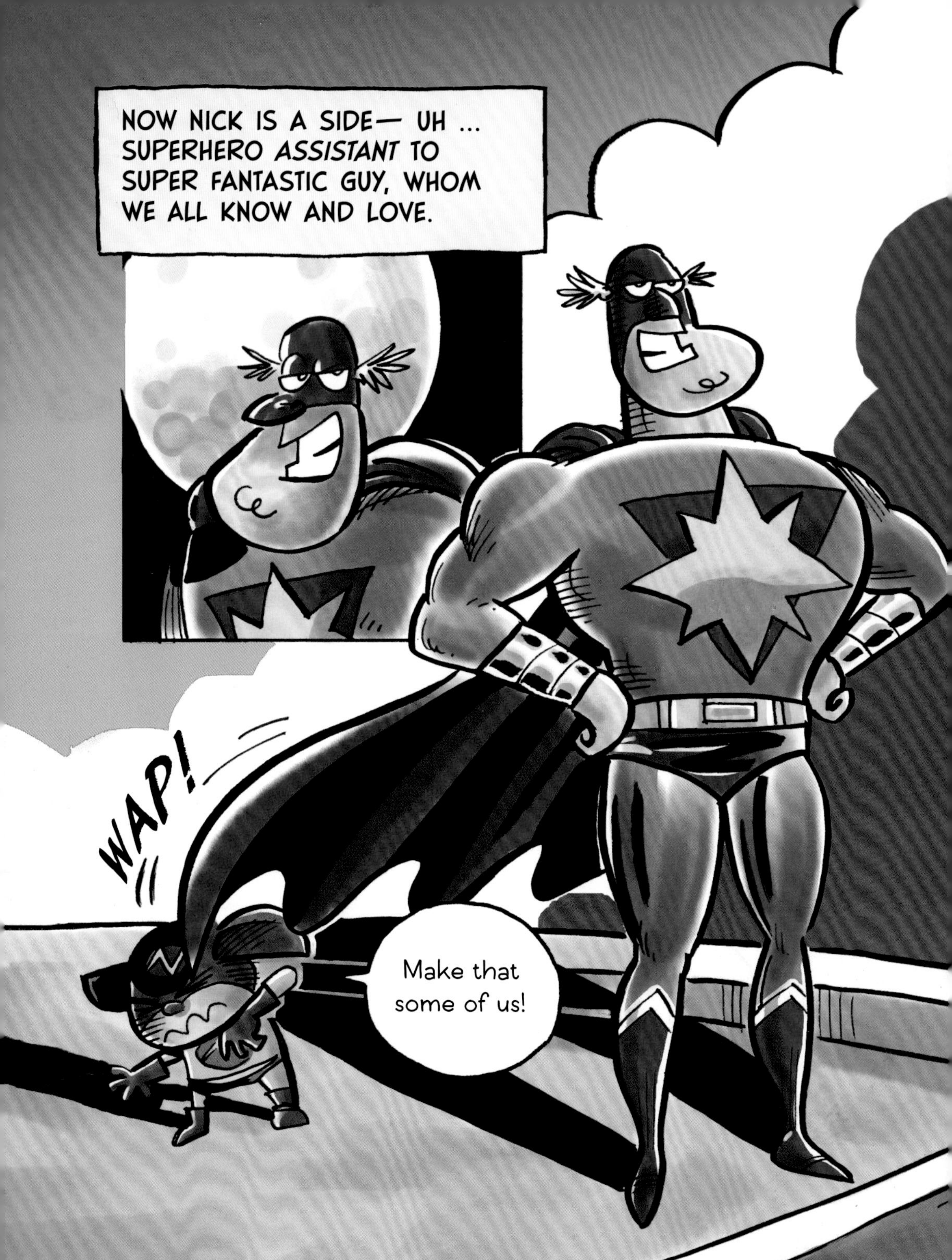
NOW NICK IS A SIDE— UH ... SUPERHERO *ASSISTANT* TO SUPER FANTASTIC GUY, WHOM WE ALL KNOW AND LOVE.
WAP!
Make that some of us!

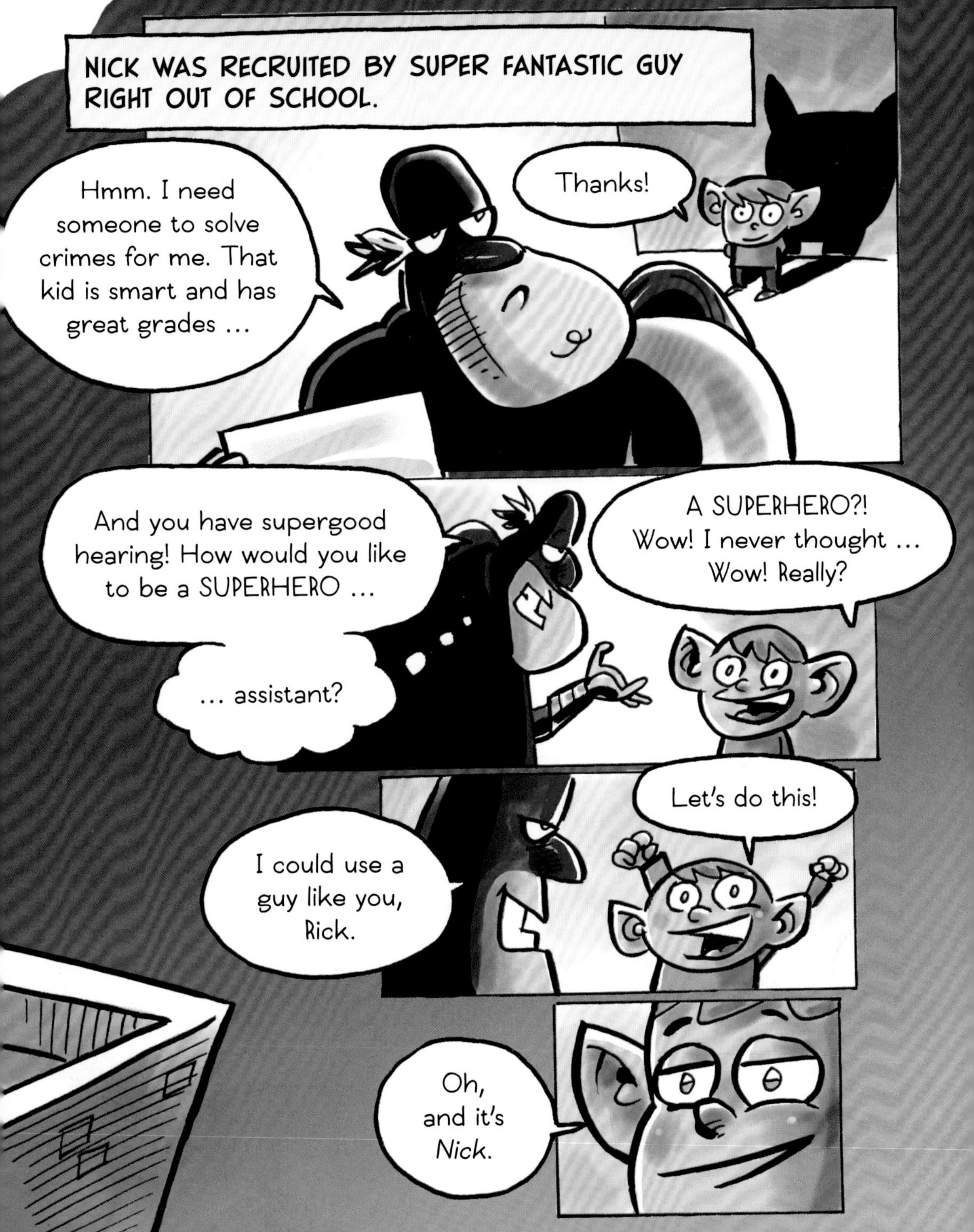
NICK WAS RECRUITED BY SUPER FANTASTIC GUY RIGHT OUT OF SCHOOL.
Hmm. I need someone to solve crimes for me. That kid is smart and has great grades ...
Thanks!
And you have supergood hearing! How would you like to be a SUPERHERO ...
... assistant?
A SUPERHERO?! Wow! I never thought ... Wow! Really?
I could use a guy like you, Rick.
Let's do this!
Oh, and it's *Nick*.

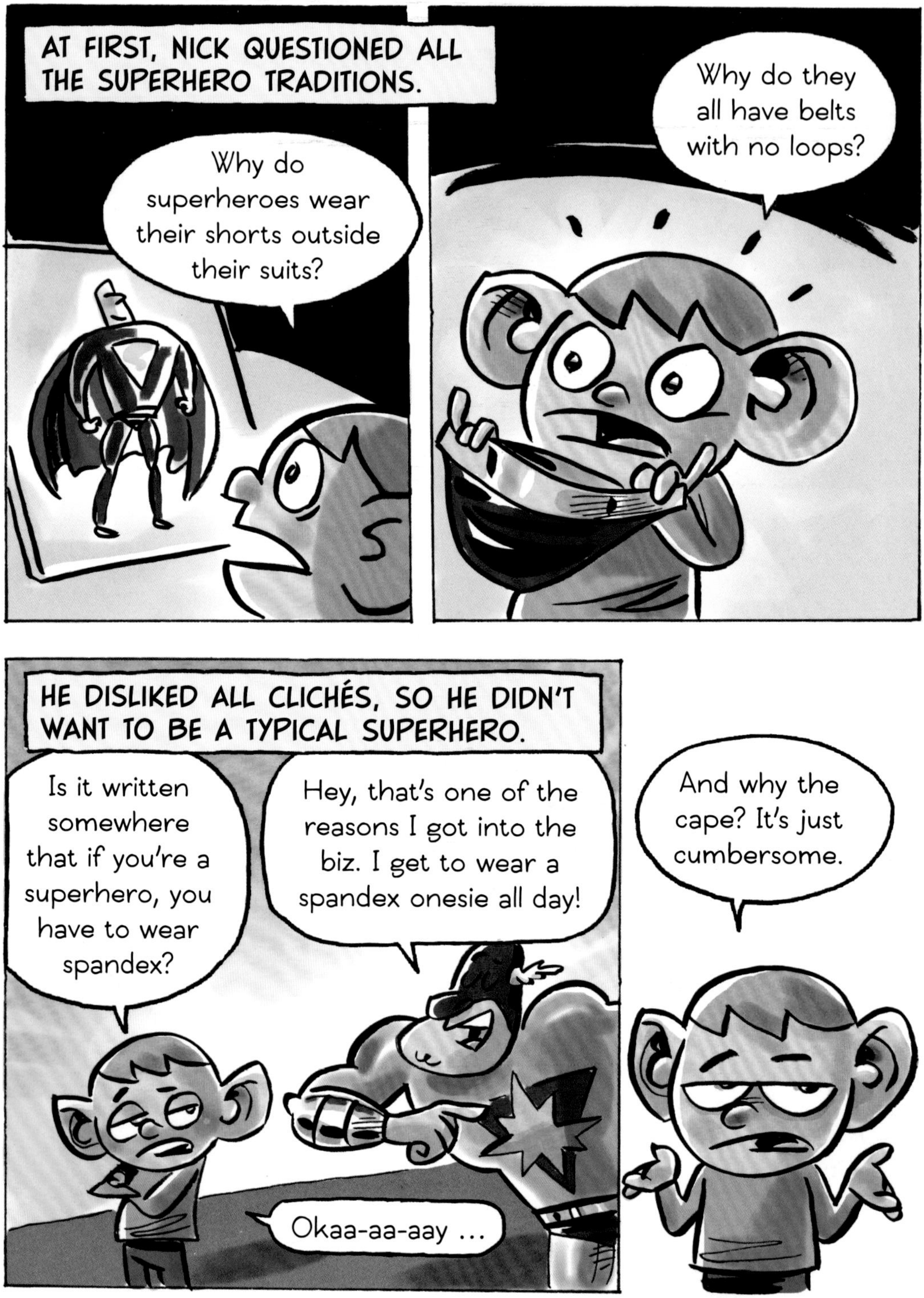
AT FIRST, NICK QUESTIONED ALL THE SUPERHERO TRADITIONS.
Why do superheroes wear their shorts outside their suits?
Why do they all have belts with no loops?
HE DISLIKED ALL CLICHÉS, SO HE DIDN'T WANT TO BE A TYPICAL SUPERHERO.
Is it written somewhere that if you're a superhero, you have to wear spandex?
Hey, that's one of the reasons I got into the biz. I get to wear a spandex onesie all day!
Okaa-aa-aay ...
And why the cape? It's just cumbersome.

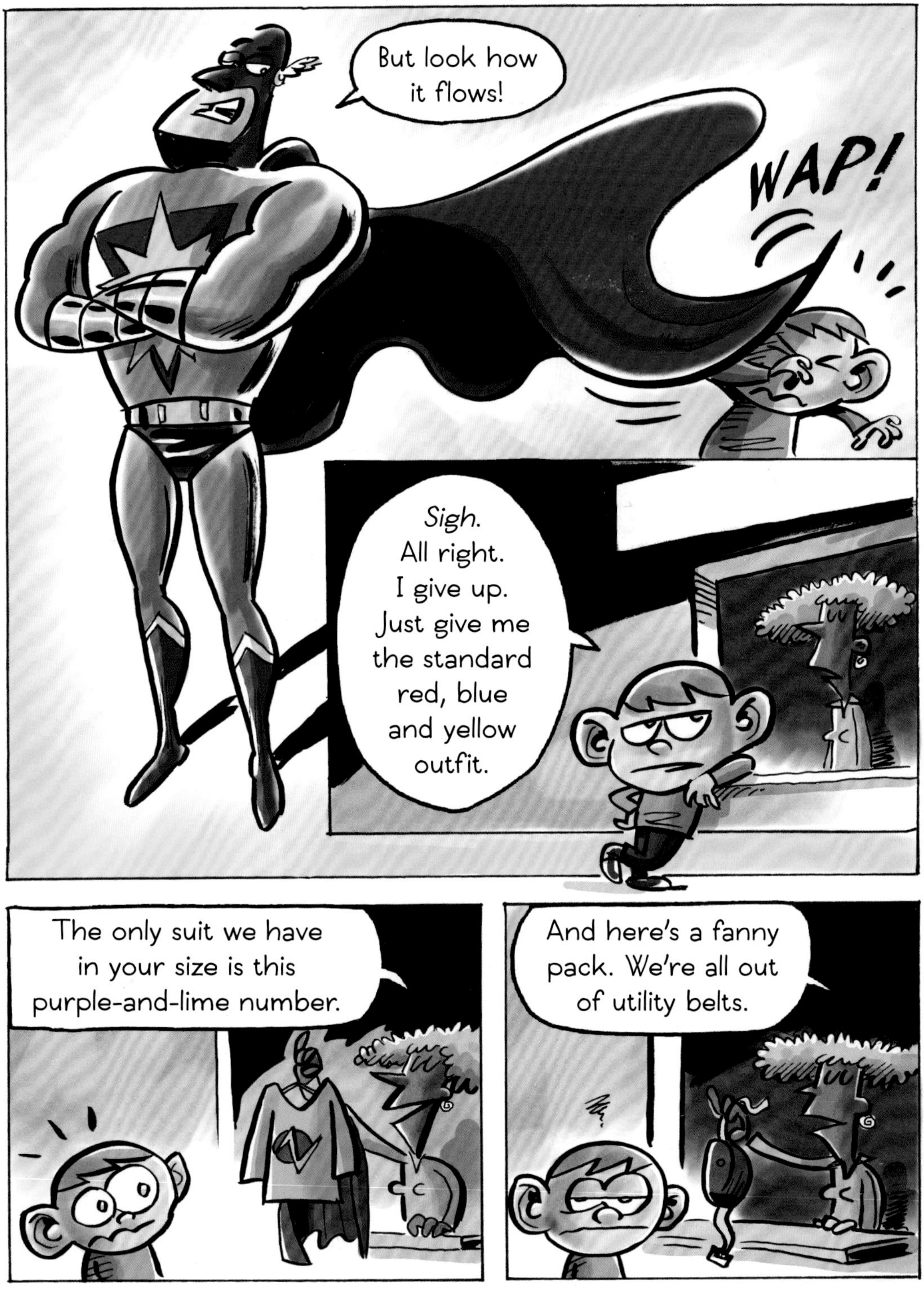
But look how it flows!
WAP!
Sigh. All right. I give up. Just give me the standard red, blue and yellow outfit.
The only suit we have in your size is this purple-and-lime number.
And here's a fanny pack. We're all out of utility belts.

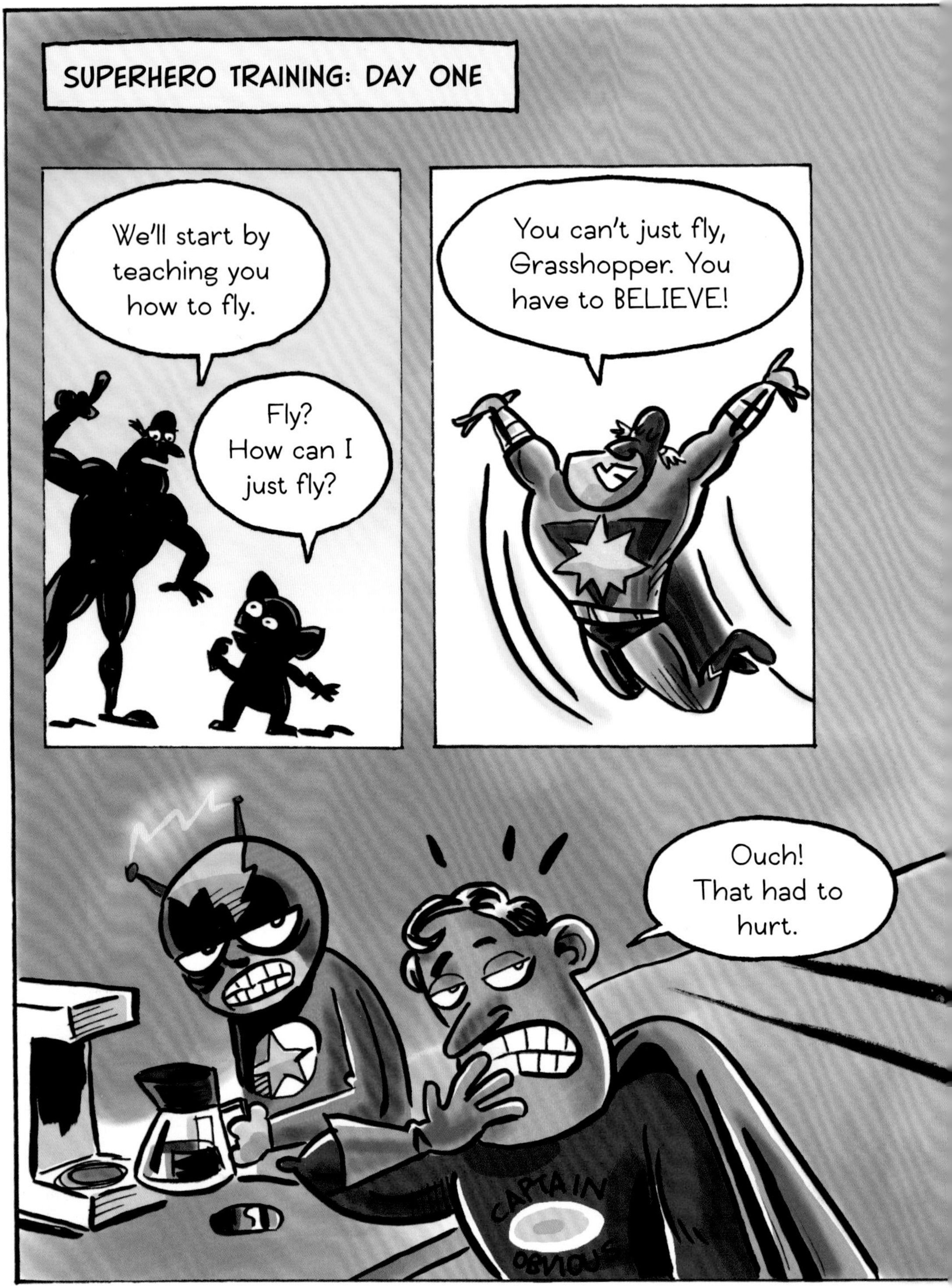
SUPERHERO TRAINING: DAY ONE
We'll start by teaching you how to fly.
Fly? How can I just fly?
You can't just fly, Grasshopper. You have to BELIEVE!
Ouch! That had to hurt.
CAPTAIN OBVIOUS

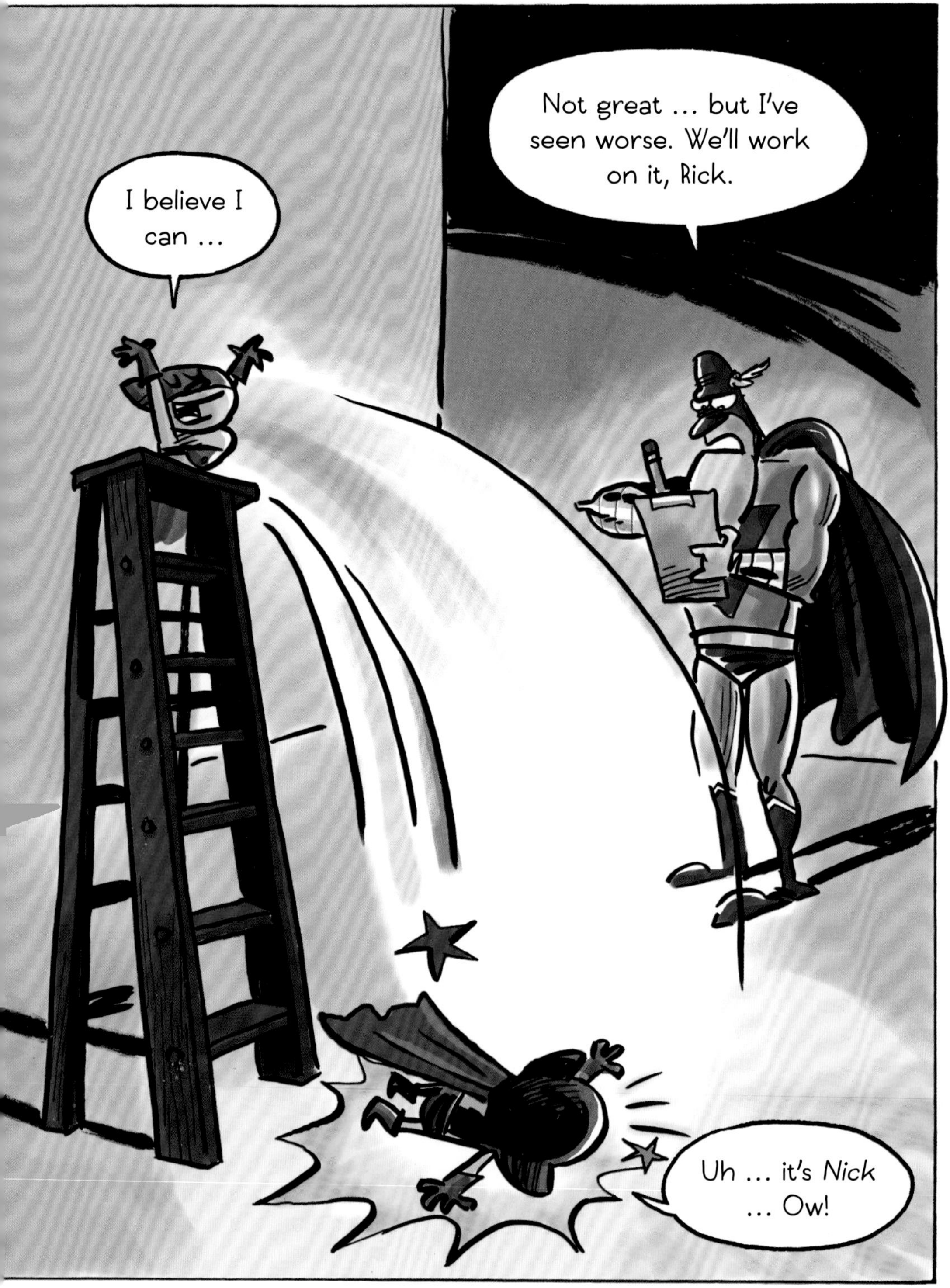
I believe I can …
Not great … but I've seen worse. We'll work on it, Rick.
Uh … it's *Nick* … Ow!

SUPERHERO TRAINING: DAY TWO

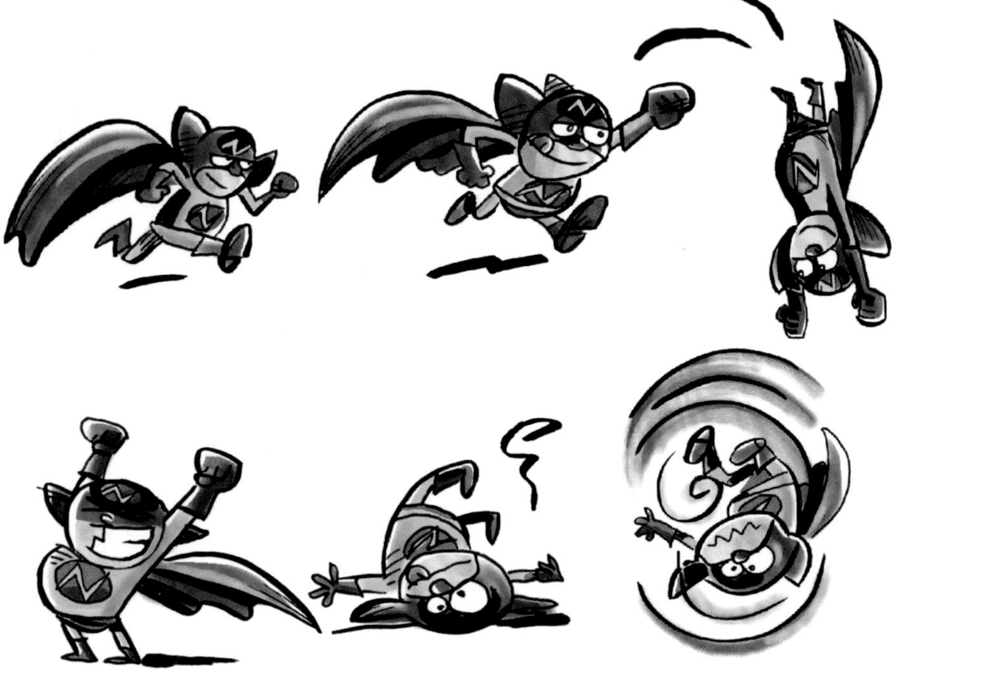

SUPERHERO TRAINING: DAY THREE

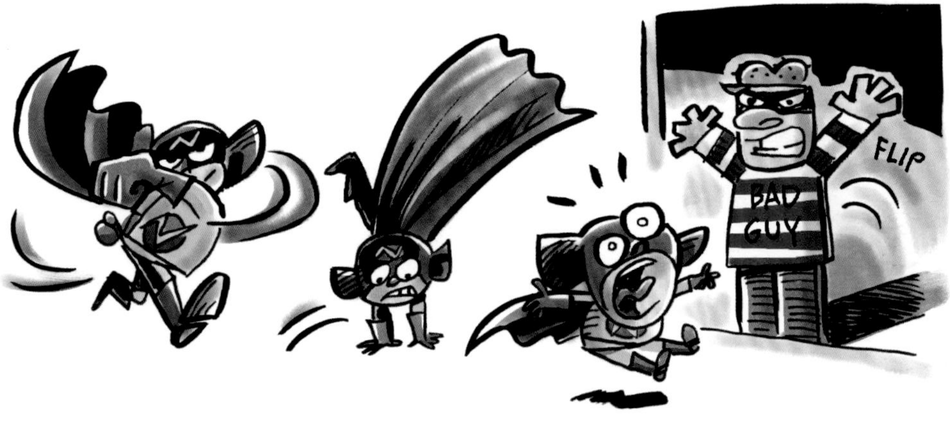
FLIP
BAD GUY

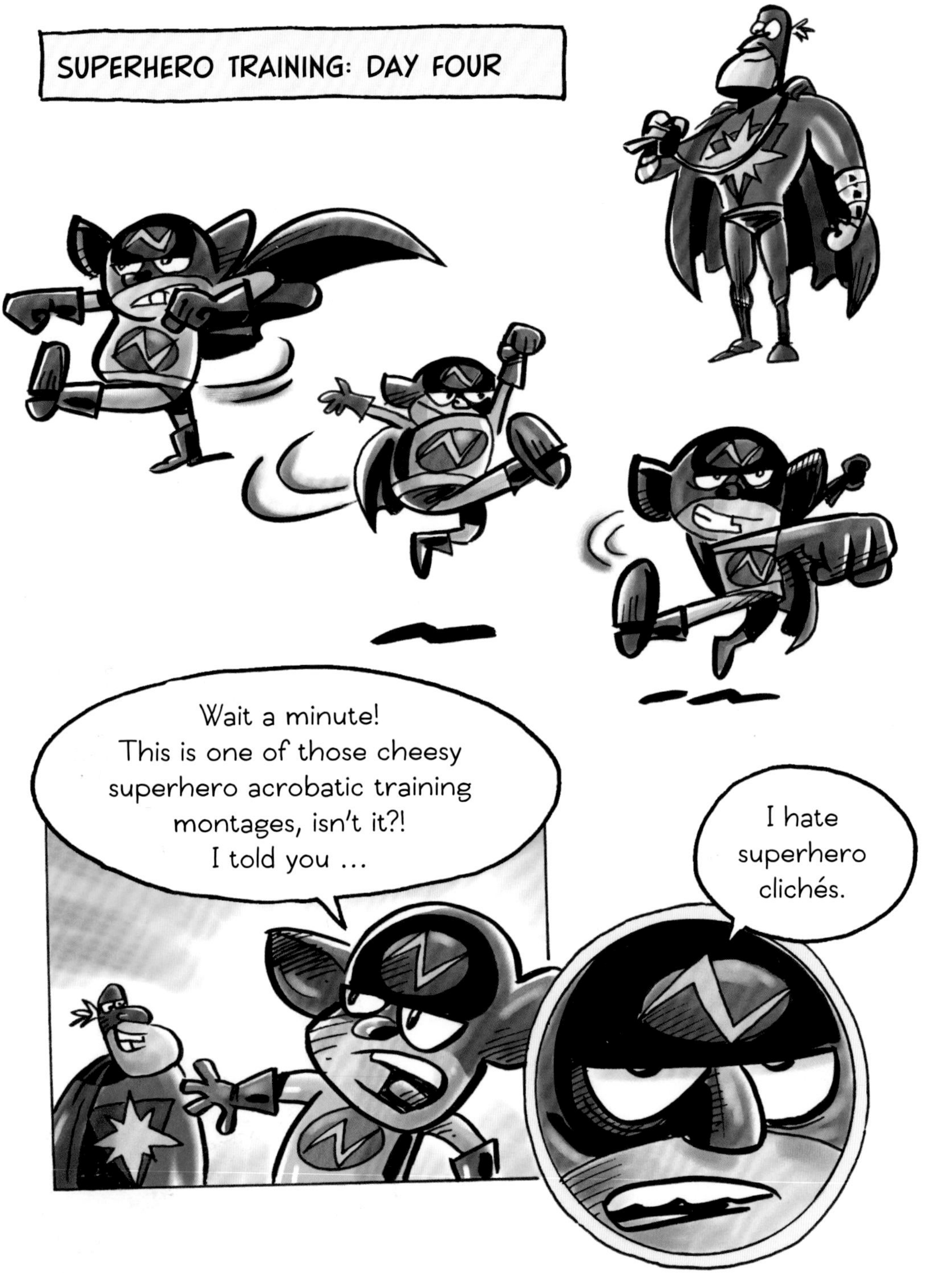
SUPERHERO TRAINING: DAY FOUR
Wait a minute! This is one of those cheesy superhero acrobatic training montages, isn't it?! I told you ...
I hate superhero clichés.

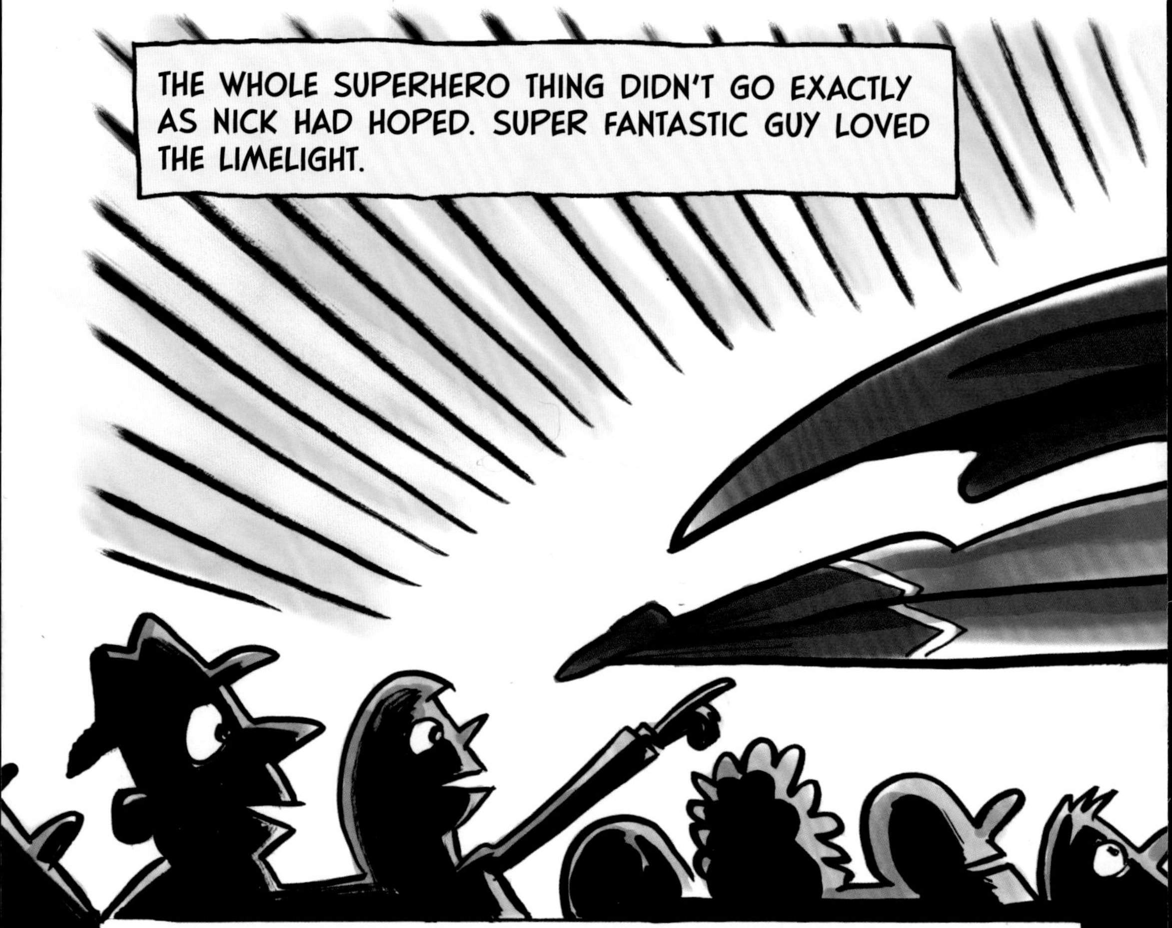
THE WHOLE SUPERHERO THING DIDN'T GO EXACTLY AS NICK HAD HOPED. SUPER FANTASTIC GUY LOVED THE LIMELIGHT.

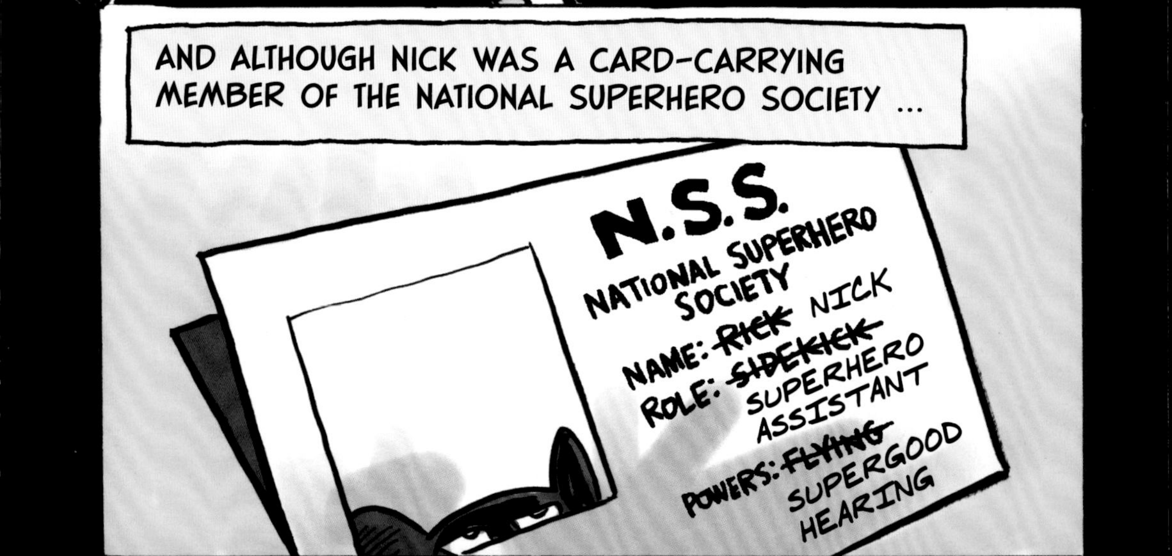
AND ALTHOUGH NICK WAS A CARD-CARRYING MEMBER OF THE NATIONAL SUPERHERO SOCIETY ...
N.S.S.
NATIONAL SUPERHERO SOCIETY
NAME: ~~RICK~~ NICK
ROLE: ~~SIDEKICK~~ SUPERHERO ASSISTANT
POWERS: ~~FLYING~~ SUPERGOOD HEARING

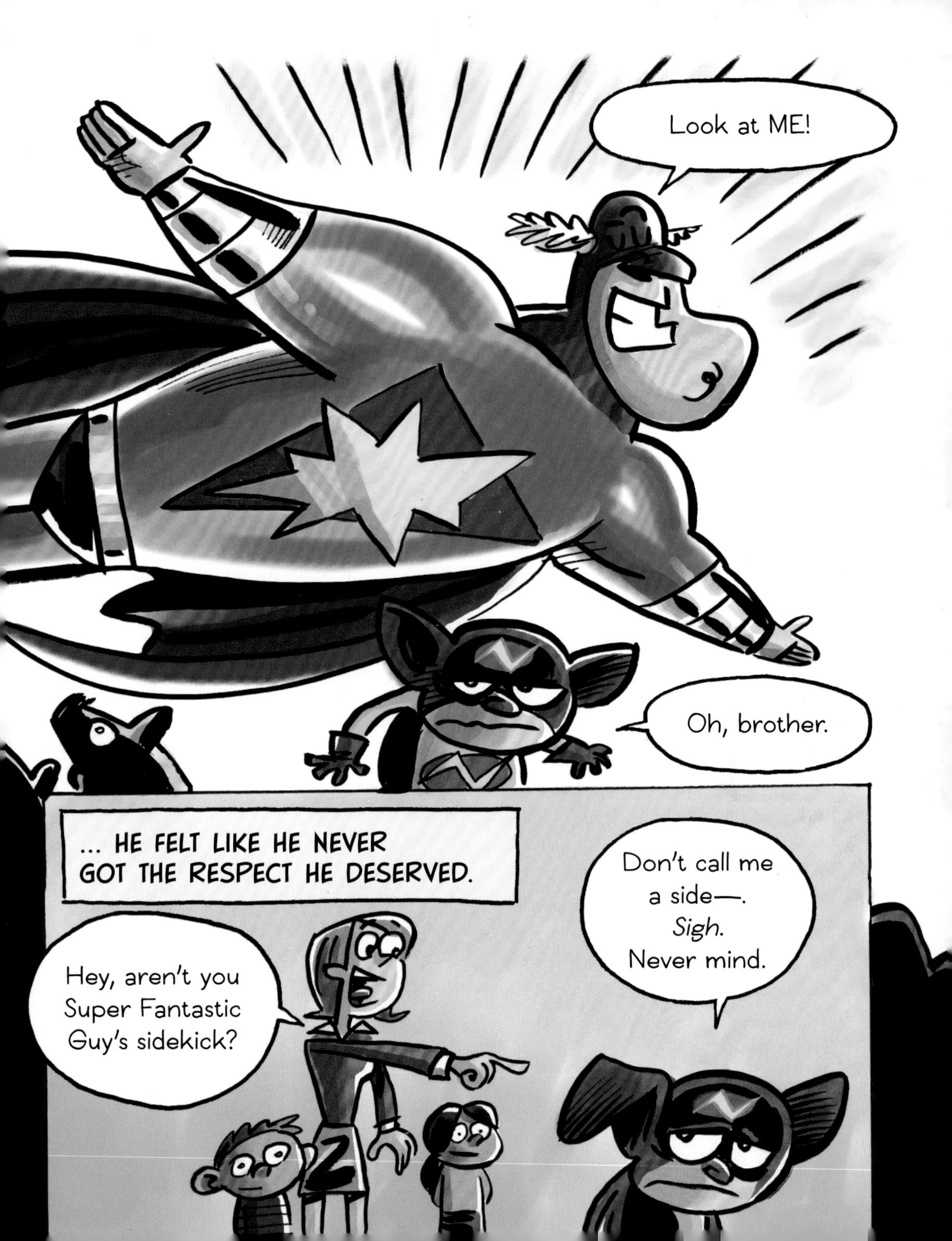
Look at ME!
Oh, brother.
... HE FELT LIKE HE NEVER GOT THE RESPECT HE DESERVED.
Hey, aren't you Super Fantastic Guy's sidekick?
Don't call me a side—. *Sigh*. Never mind.

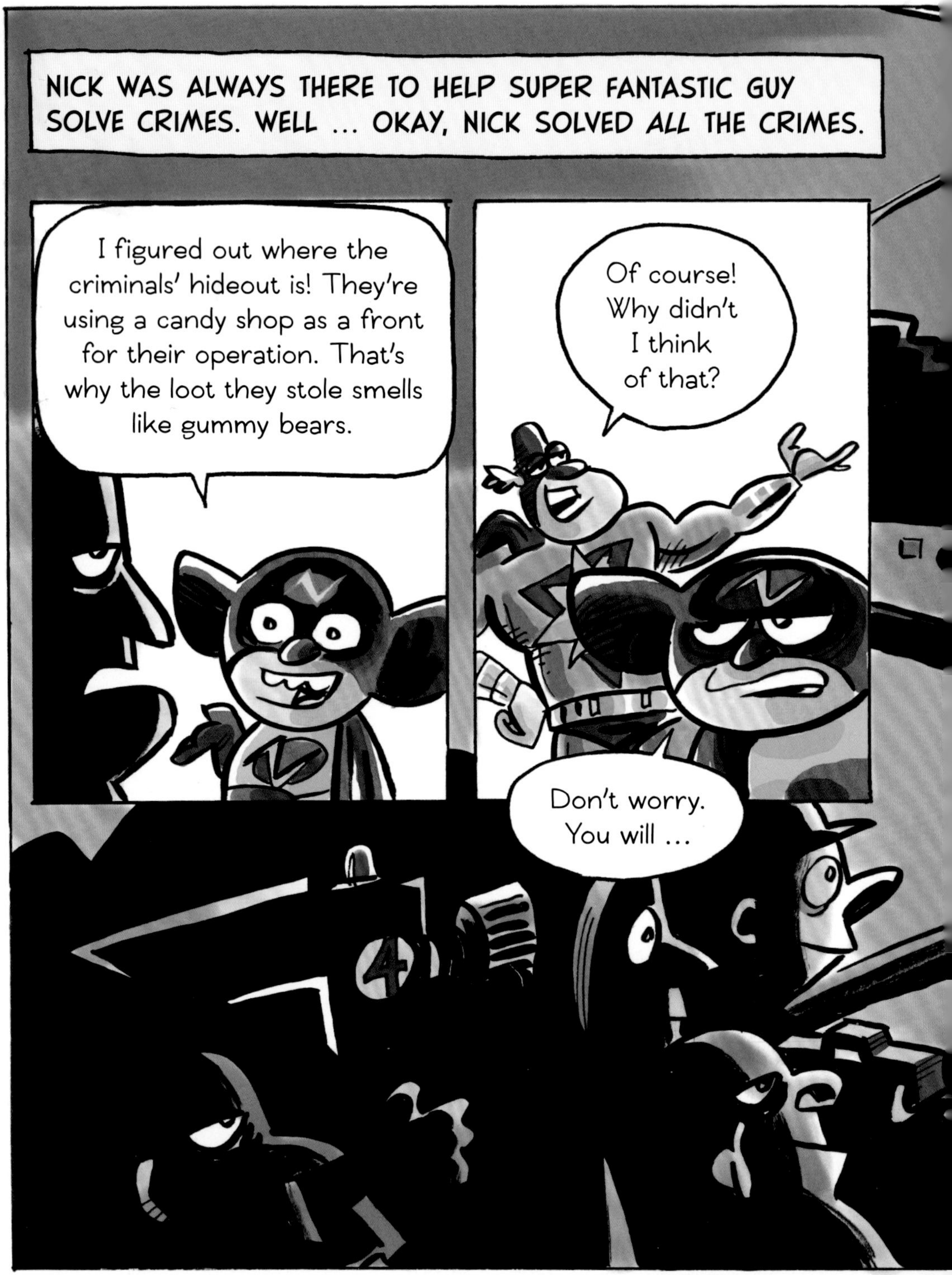
NICK WAS ALWAYS THERE TO HELP SUPER FANTASTIC GUY SOLVE CRIMES. WELL ... OKAY, NICK SOLVED *ALL* THE CRIMES.
I figured out where the criminals' hideout is! They're using a candy shop as a front for their operation. That's why the loot they stole smells like gummy bears.
Of course! Why didn't I think of that?
Don't worry. You will ...

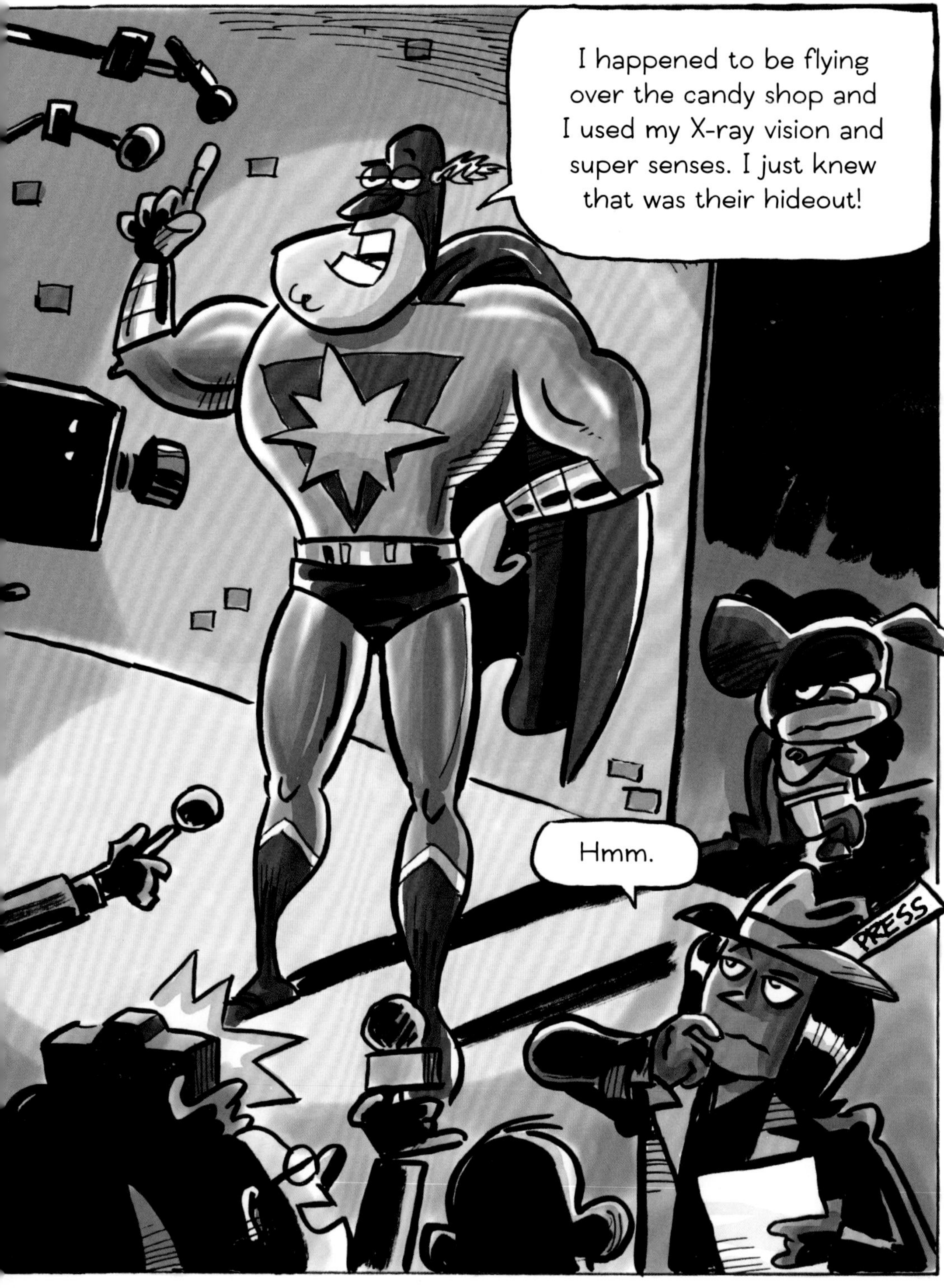
I happened to be flying over the candy shop and I used my X-ray vision and super senses. I just knew that was their hideout!
Hmm.
PRESS

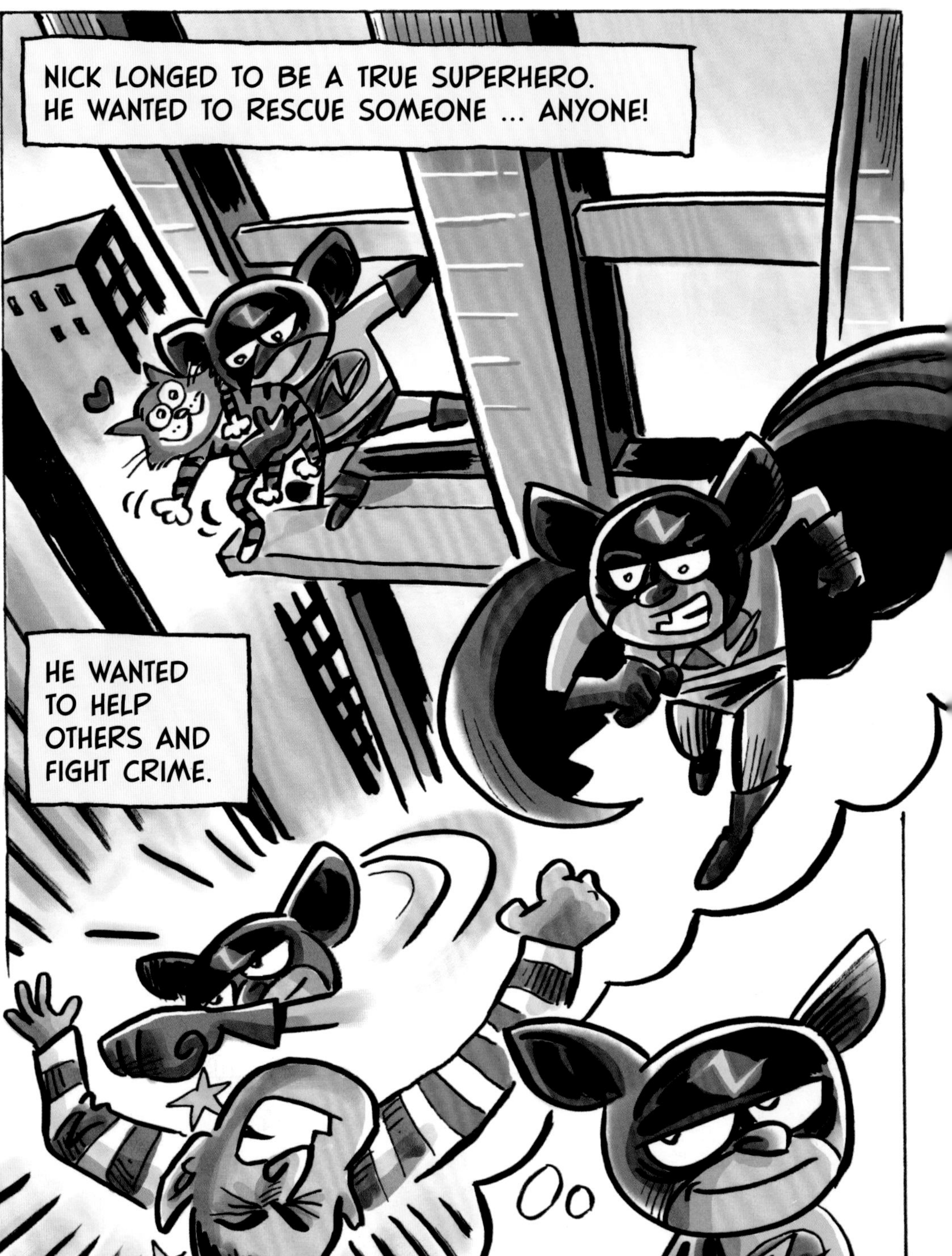
NICK LONGED TO BE A TRUE SUPERHERO. HE WANTED TO RESCUE SOMEONE ... ANYONE!
HE WANTED TO HELP OTHERS AND FIGHT CRIME.
OO

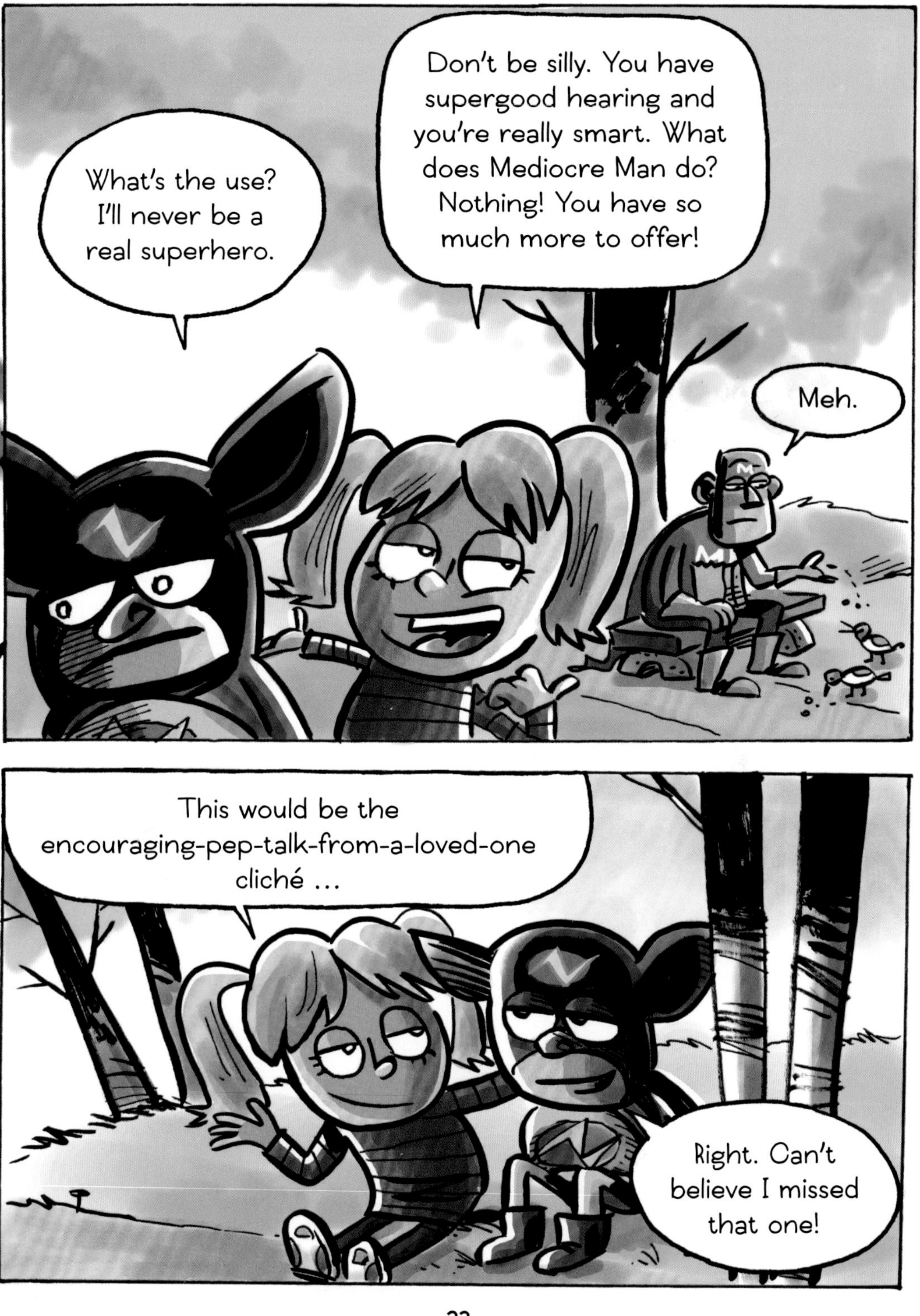
What's the use? I'll never be a real superhero.
Don't be silly. You have supergood hearing and you're really smart. What does Mediocre Man do? Nothing! You have so much more to offer!
Meh.
This would be the encouraging-pep-talk-from-a-loved-one cliché …
Right. Can't believe I missed that one!

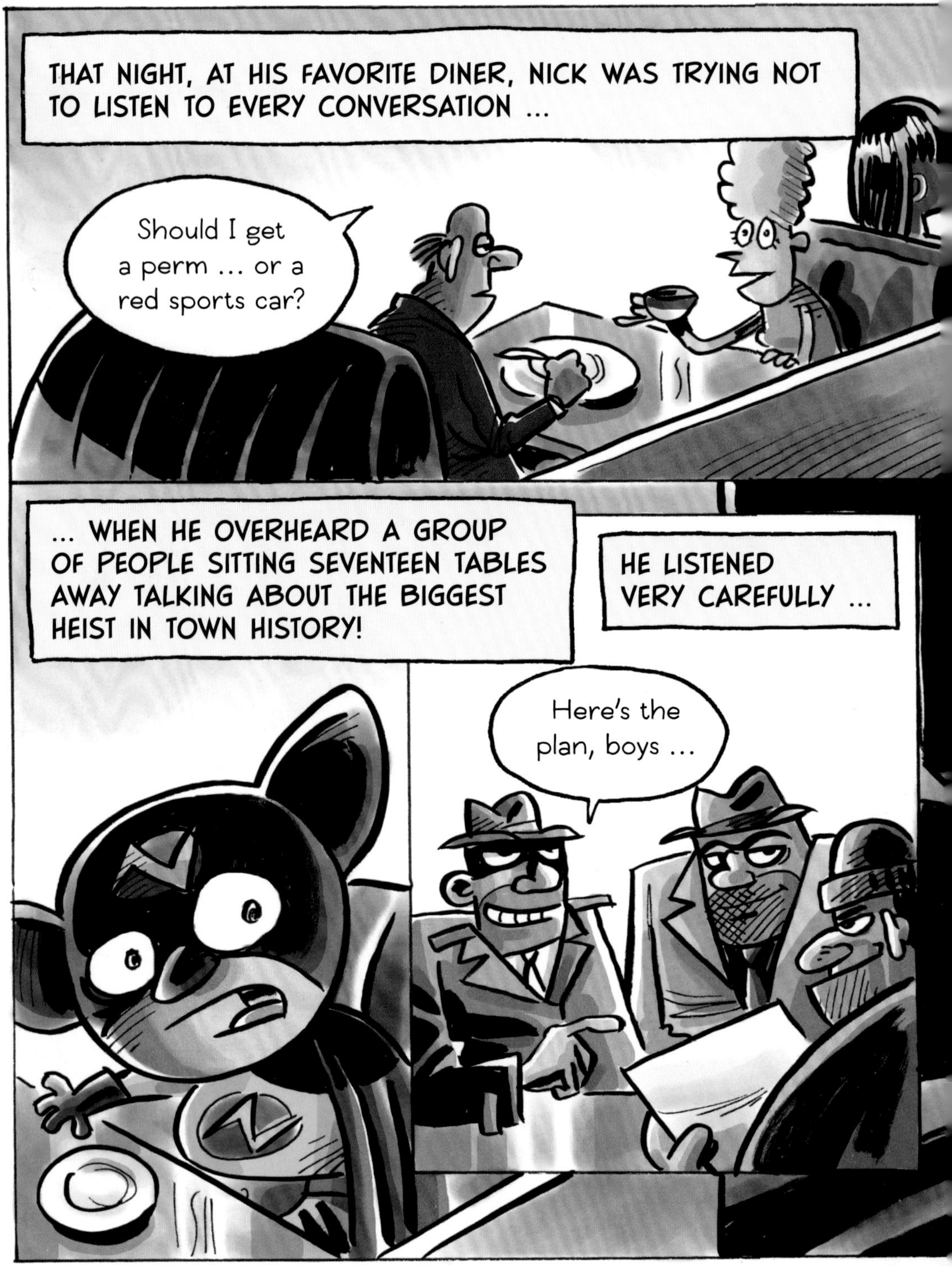
THAT NIGHT, AT HIS FAVORITE DINER, NICK WAS TRYING NOT TO LISTEN TO EVERY CONVERSATION ...
Should I get a perm ... or a red sports car?
... WHEN HE OVERHEARD A GROUP OF PEOPLE SITTING SEVENTEEN TABLES AWAY TALKING ABOUT THE BIGGEST HEIST IN TOWN HISTORY!
HE LISTENED VERY CAREFULLY ...
Here's the plan, boys ...

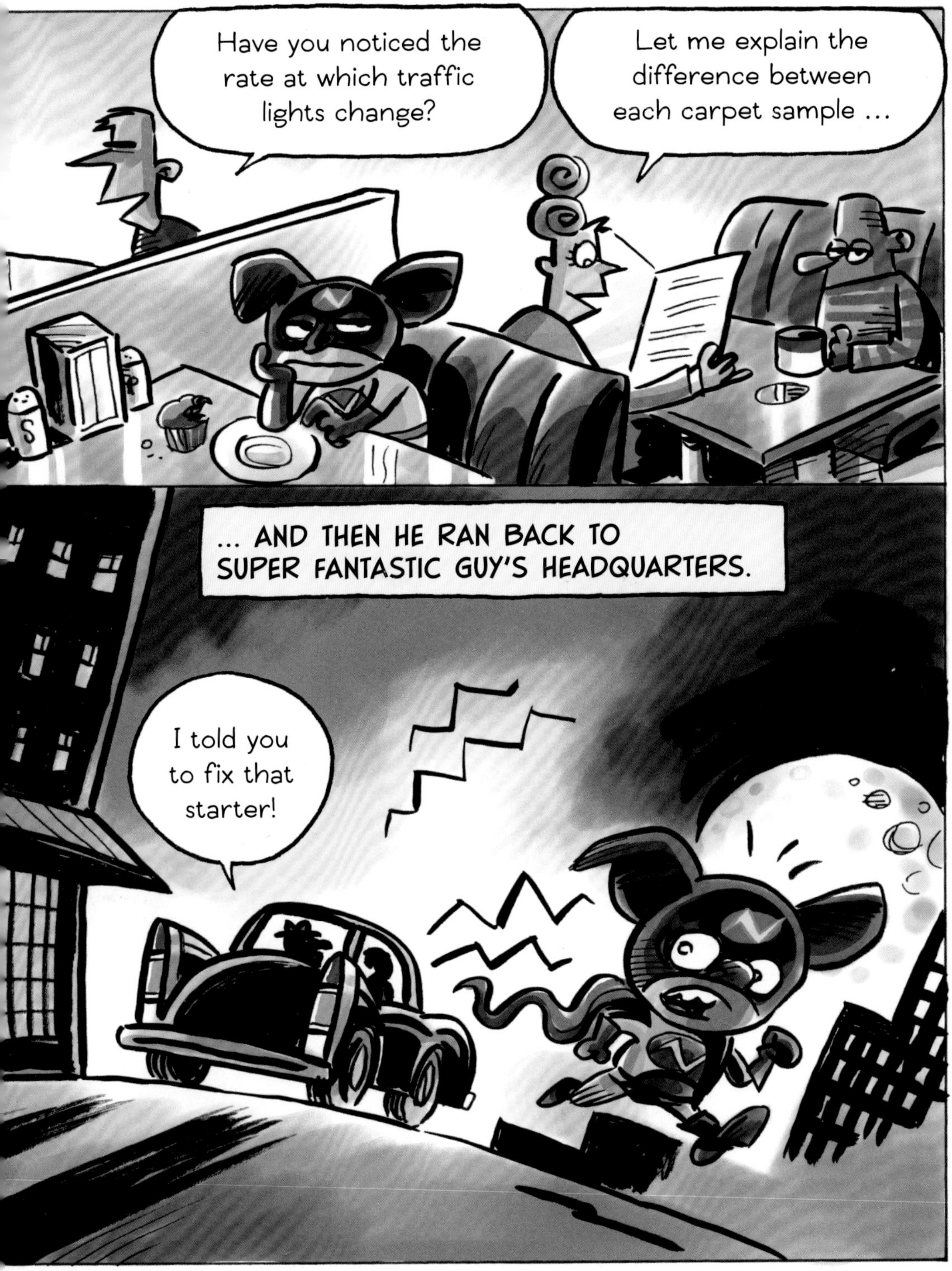
Have you noticed the rate at which traffic lights change?
Let me explain the difference between each carpet sample ...
... AND THEN HE RAN BACK TO SUPER FANTASTIC GUY'S HEADQUARTERS.
I told you to fix that starter!

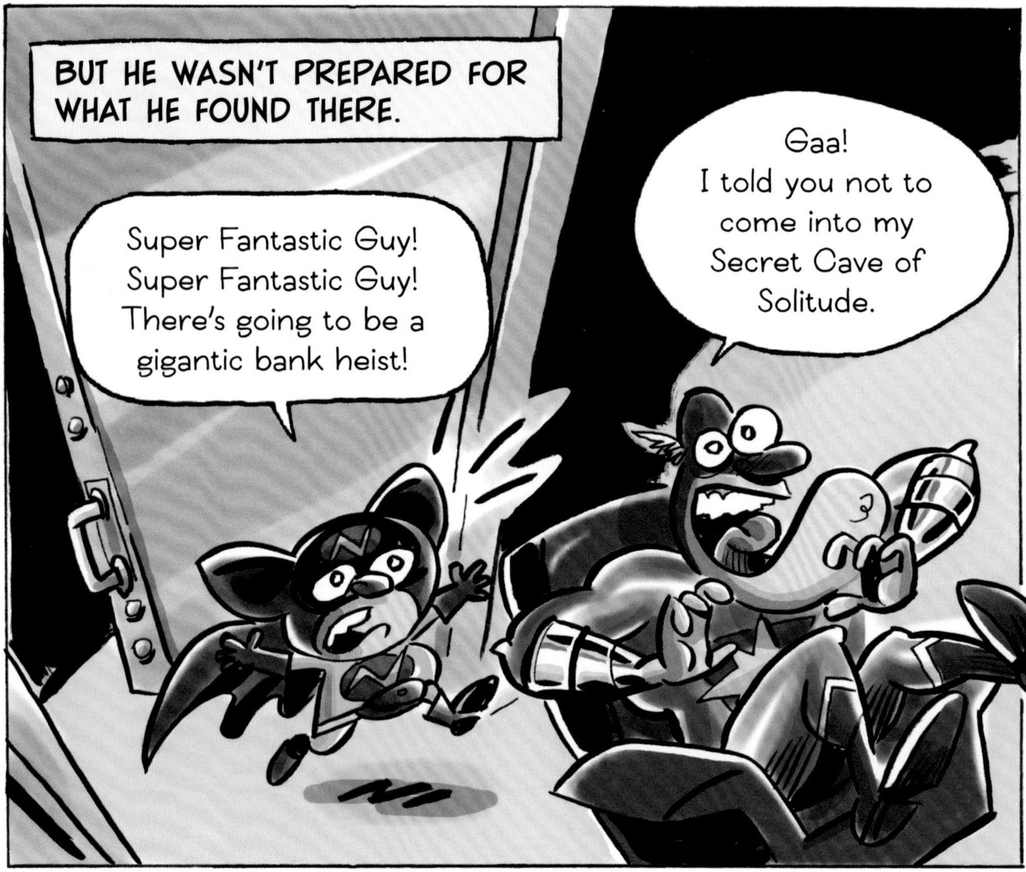
BUT HE WASN'T PREPARED FOR WHAT HE FOUND THERE.
Super Fantastic Guy! Super Fantastic Guy! There's going to be a gigantic bank heist!
Gaa! I told you not to come into my Secret Cave of Solitude.

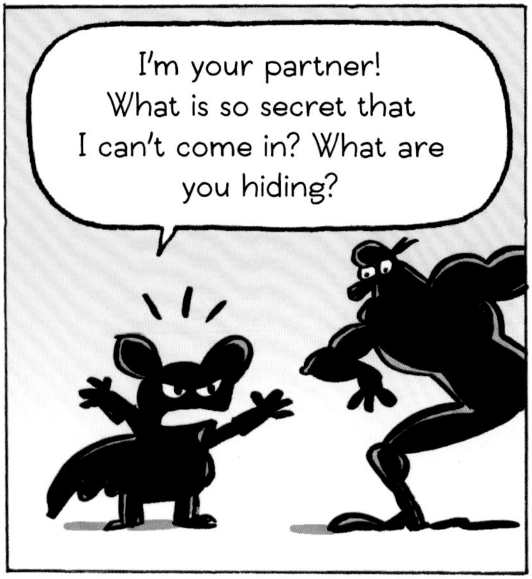
I'm your partner! What is so secret that I can't come in? What are you hiding?

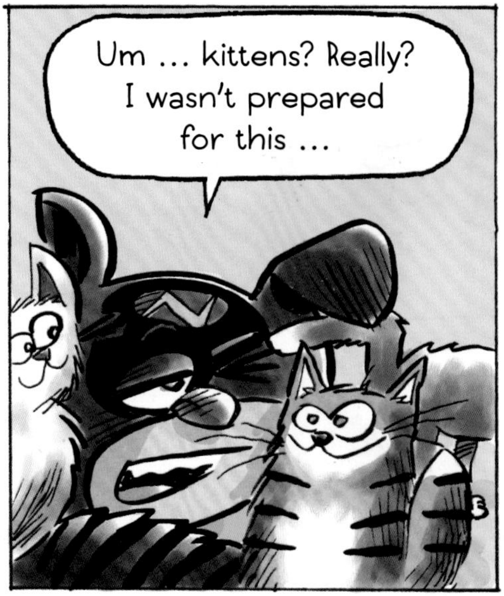
Um ... kittens? Really? I wasn't prepared for this ...

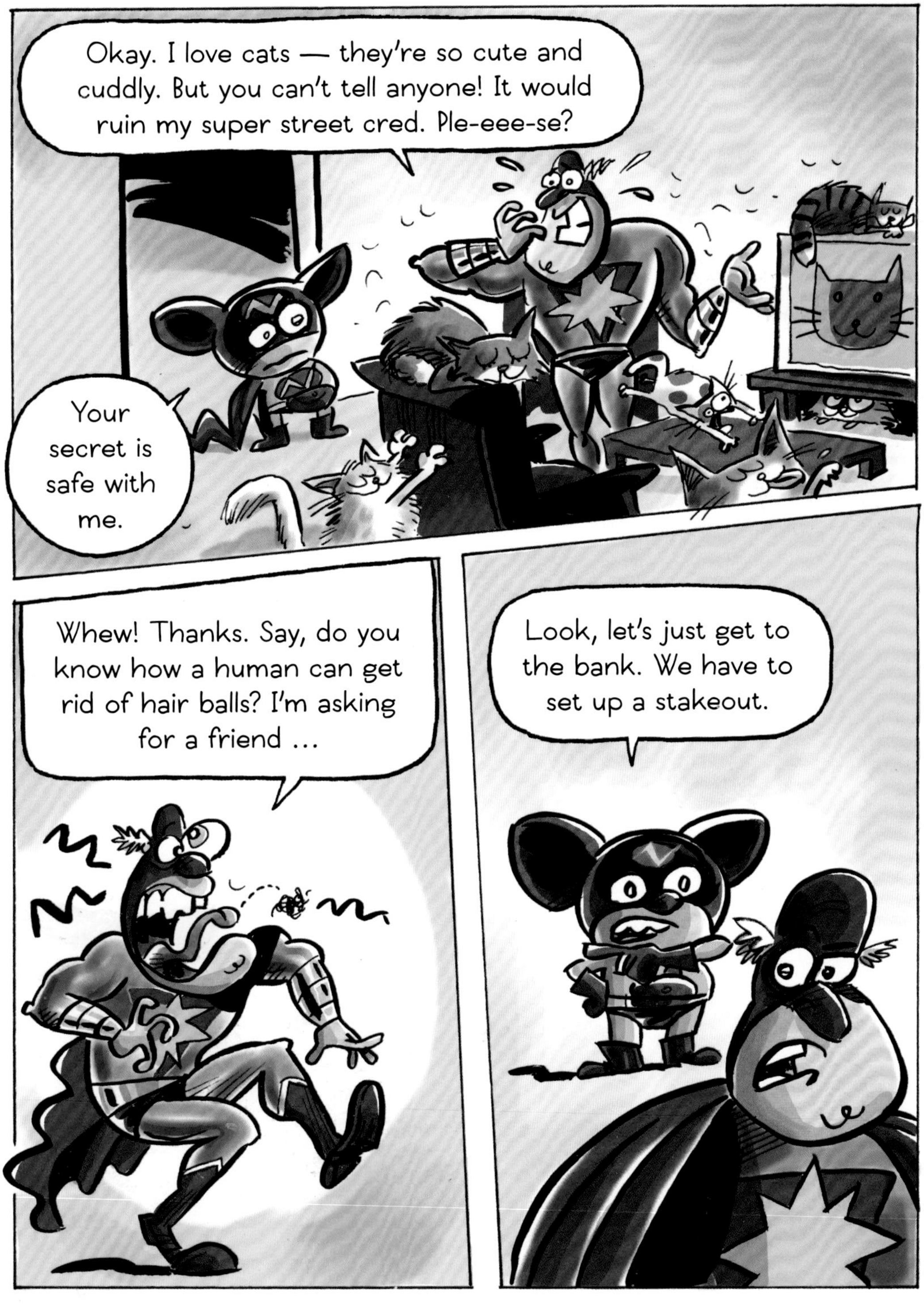
Okay. I love cats — they're so cute and cuddly. But you can't tell anyone! It would ruin my super street cred. Ple-eee-se?
Your secret is safe with me.
Whew! Thanks. Say, do you know how a human can get rid of hair balls? I'm asking for a friend …
Look, let's just get to the bank. We have to set up a stakeout.

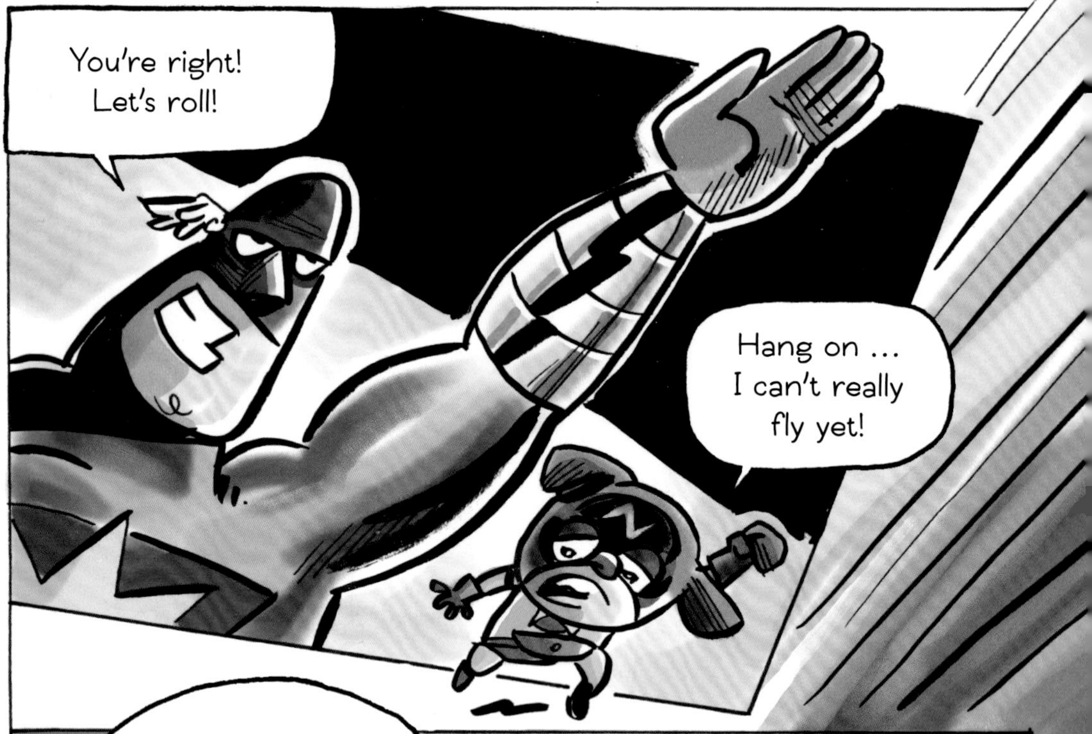
You're right! Let's roll!
Hang on ... I can't really fly yet!

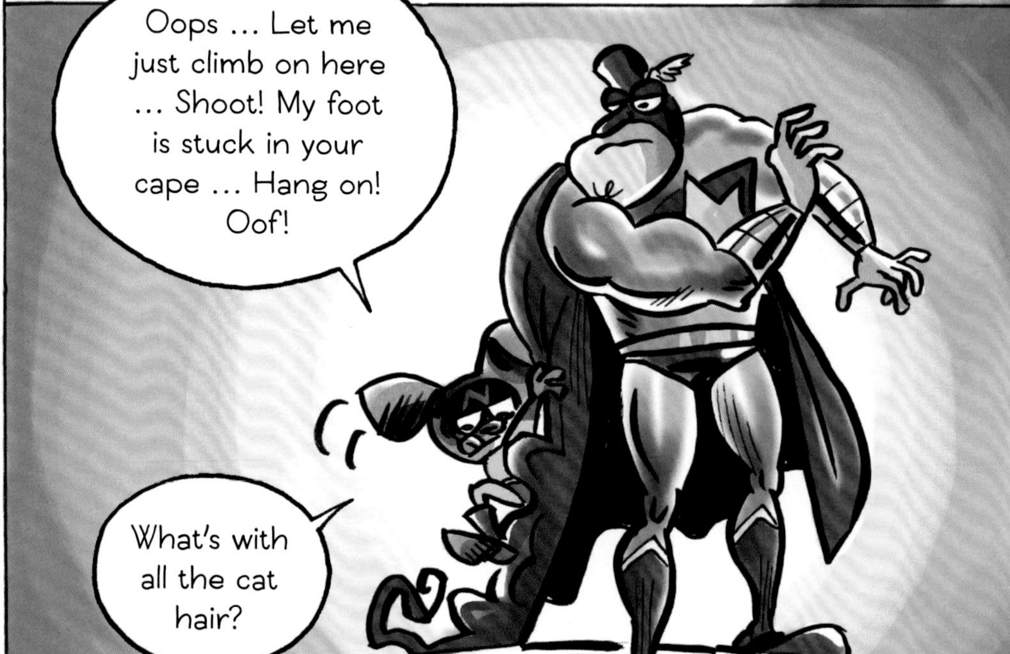
Oops ... Let me just climb on here ... Shoot! My foot is stuck in your cape ... Hang on! Oof!
What's with all the cat hair?

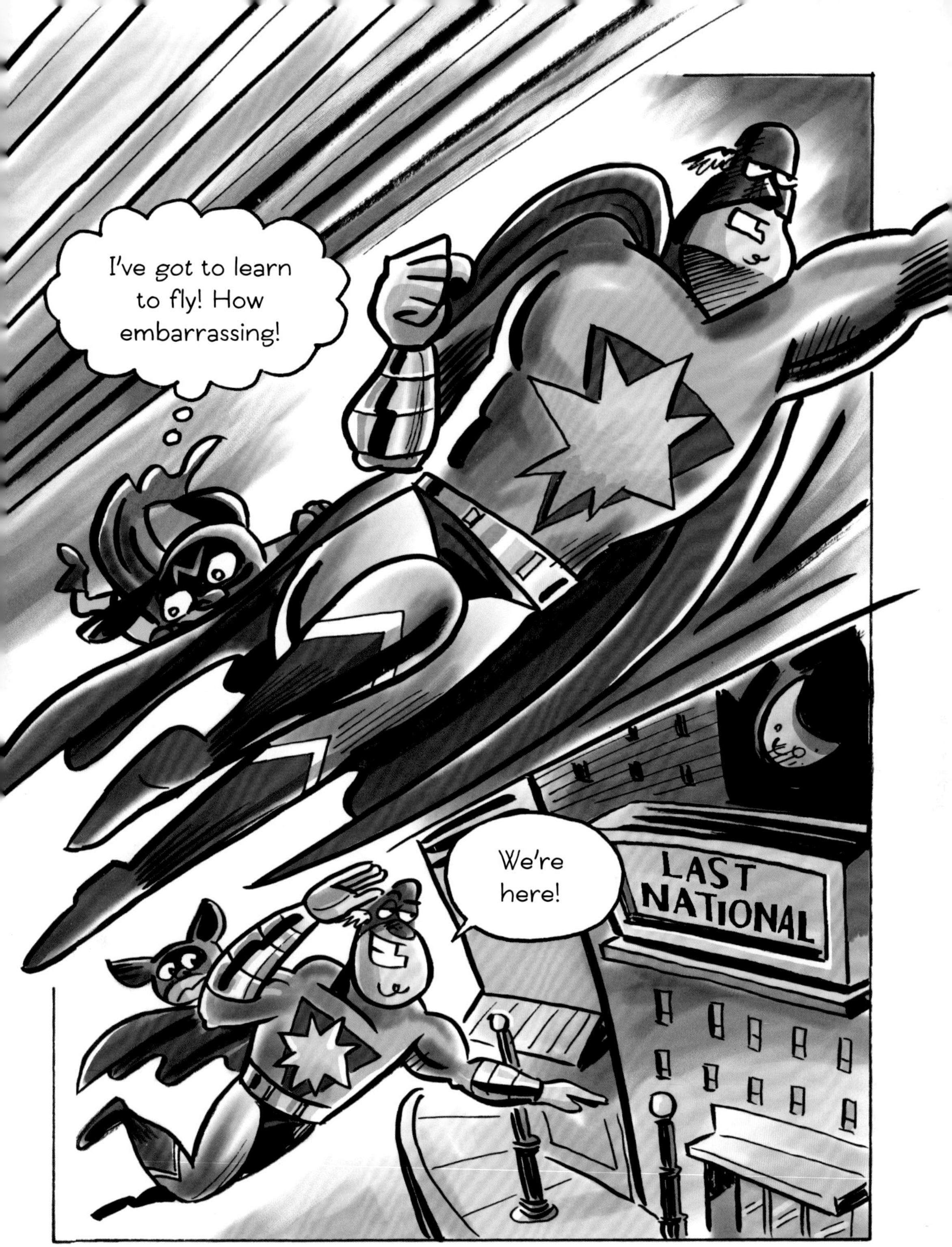
I've got to learn to fly! How embarrassing!
We're here!
LAST NATIONAL

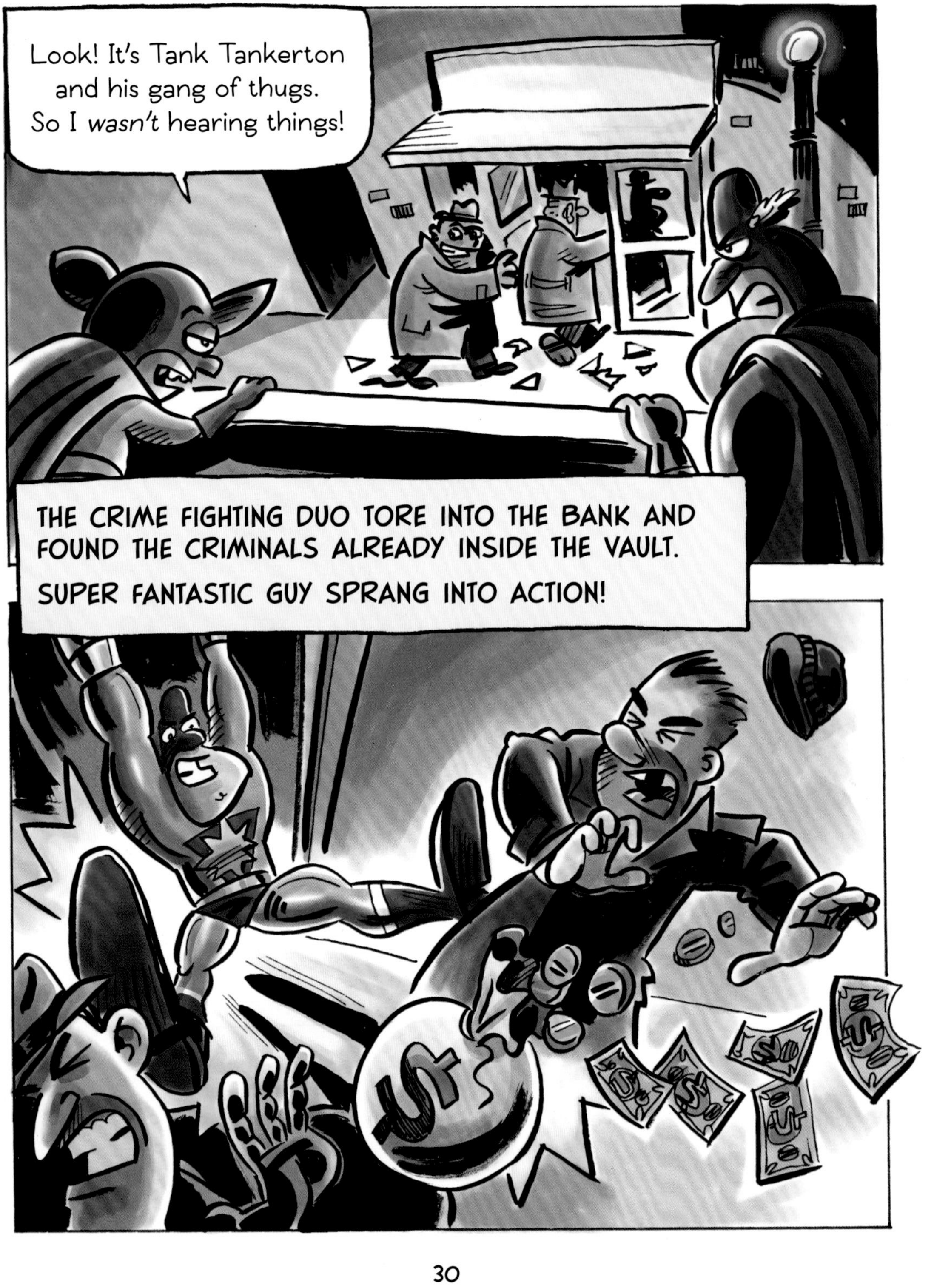
Look! It's Tank Tankerton and his gang of thugs. So I *wasn't* hearing things!
THE CRIME FIGHTING DUO TORE INTO THE BANK AND FOUND THE CRIMINALS ALREADY INSIDE THE VAULT.
SUPER FANTASTIC GUY SPRANG INTO ACTION!

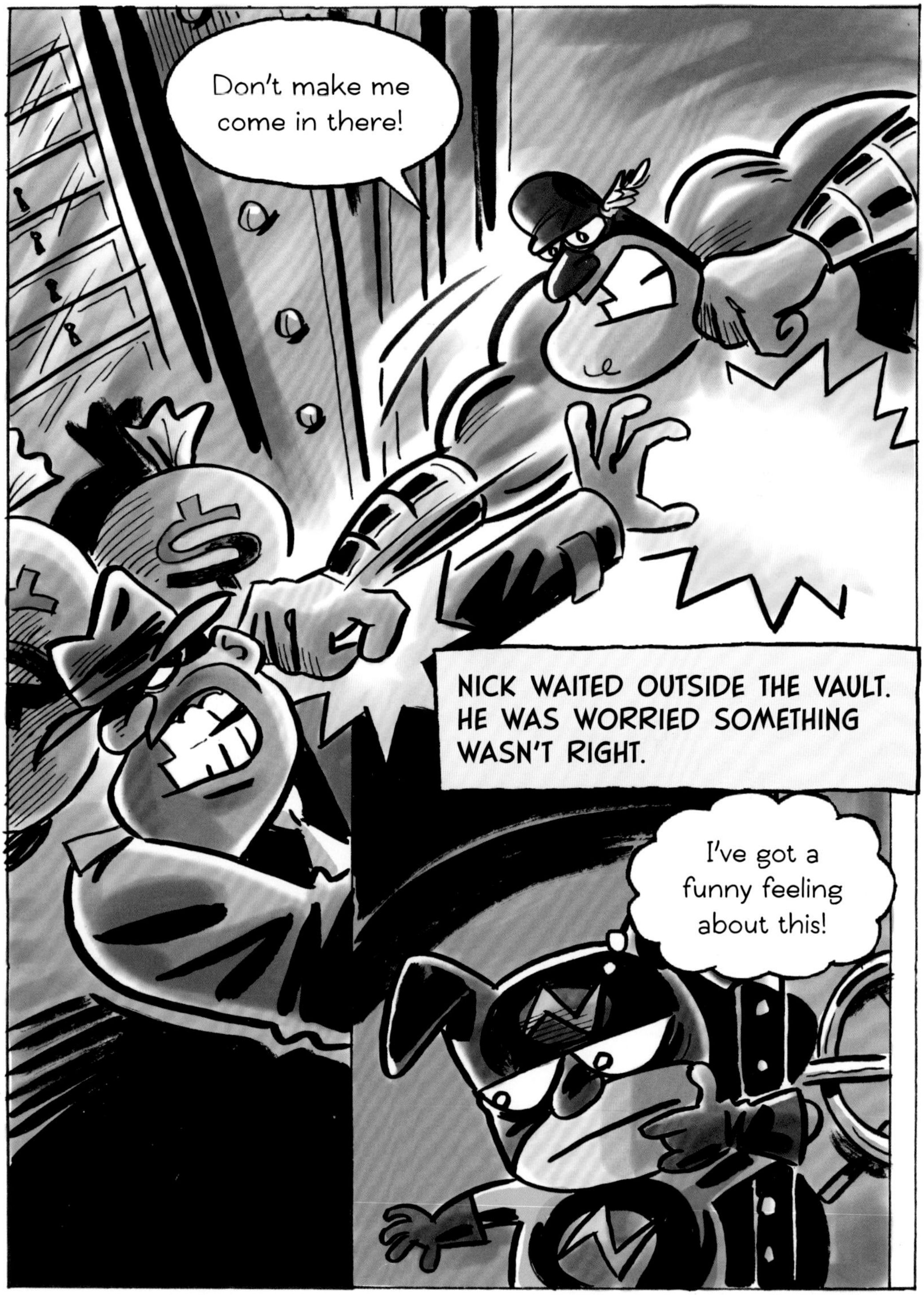
Don't make me come in there!
NICK WAITED OUTSIDE THE VAULT. HE WAS WORRIED SOMETHING WASN'T RIGHT.
I've got a funny feeling about this!

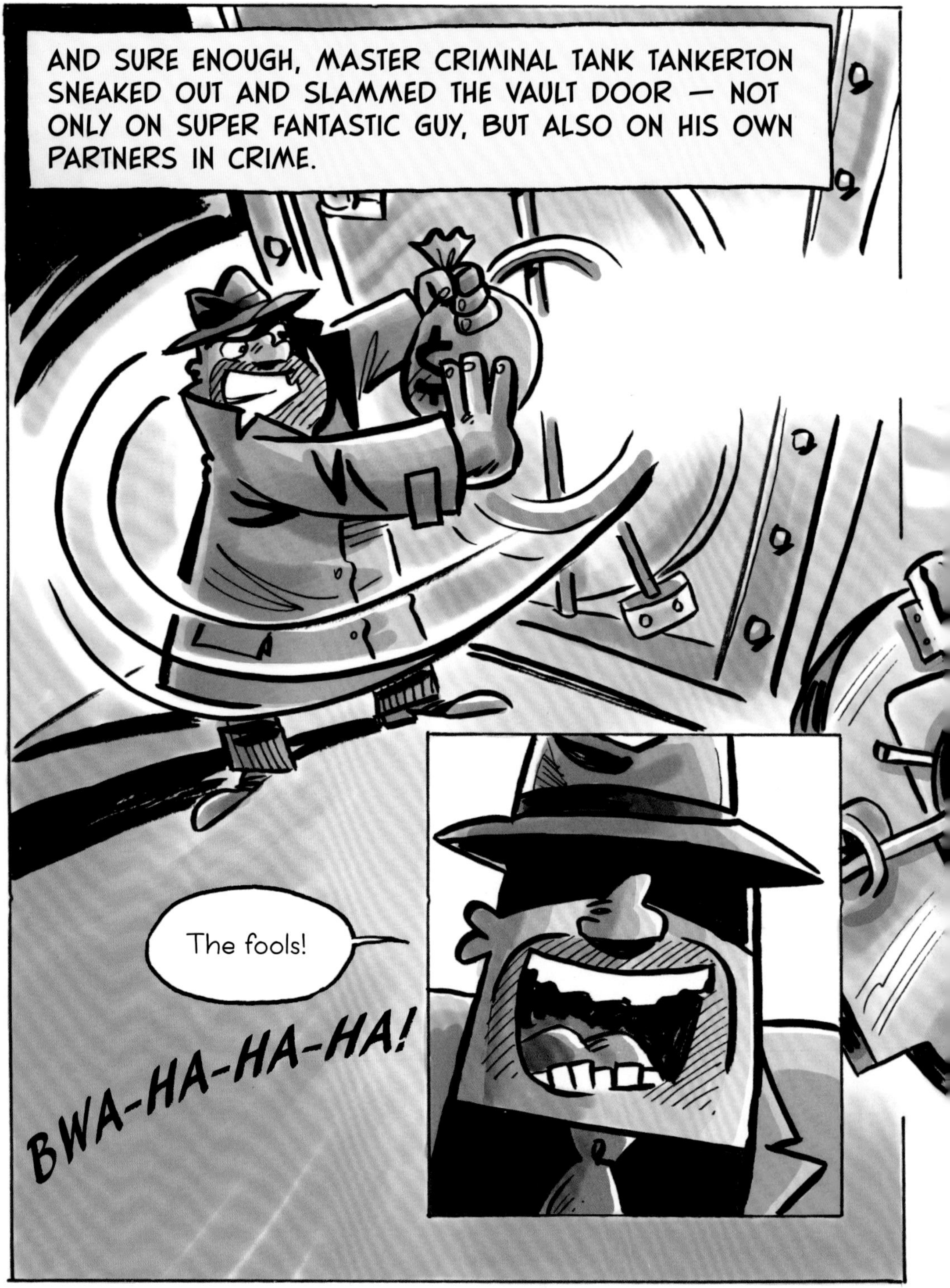
AND SURE ENOUGH, MASTER CRIMINAL TANK TANKERTON SNEAKED OUT AND SLAMMED THE VAULT DOOR — NOT ONLY ON SUPER FANTASTIC GUY, BUT ALSO ON HIS OWN PARTNERS IN CRIME.
The fools!
BWA-HA-HA-HA-HA!

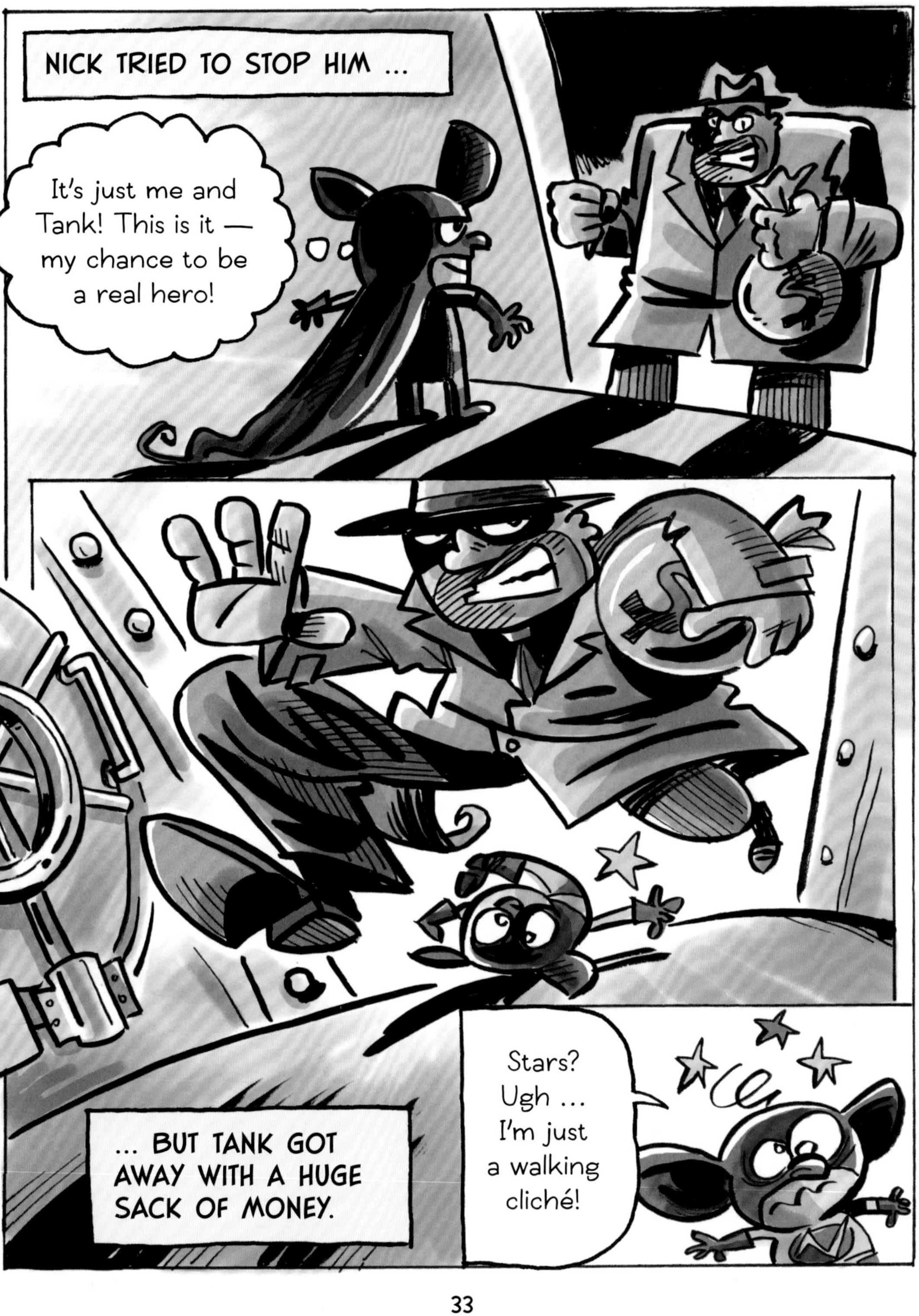
NICK TRIED TO STOP HIM ...
It's just me and Tank! This is it — my chance to be a real hero!
... BUT TANK GOT AWAY WITH A HUGE SACK OF MONEY.
Stars? Ugh ... I'm just a walking cliché!

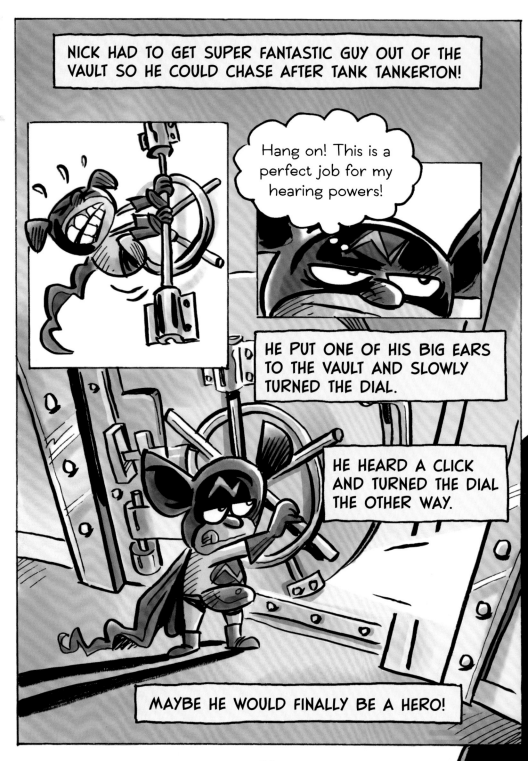

NICK HAD TO GET SUPER FANTASTIC GUY OUT OF THE VAULT SO HE COULD CHASE AFTER TANK TANKERTON!

Hang on! This is a perfect job for my hearing powers!

HE PUT ONE OF HIS BIG EARS TO THE VAULT AND SLOWLY TURNED THE DIAL.

HE HEARD A CLICK AND TURNED THE DIAL THE OTHER WAY.

MAYBE HE WOULD FINALLY BE A HERO!

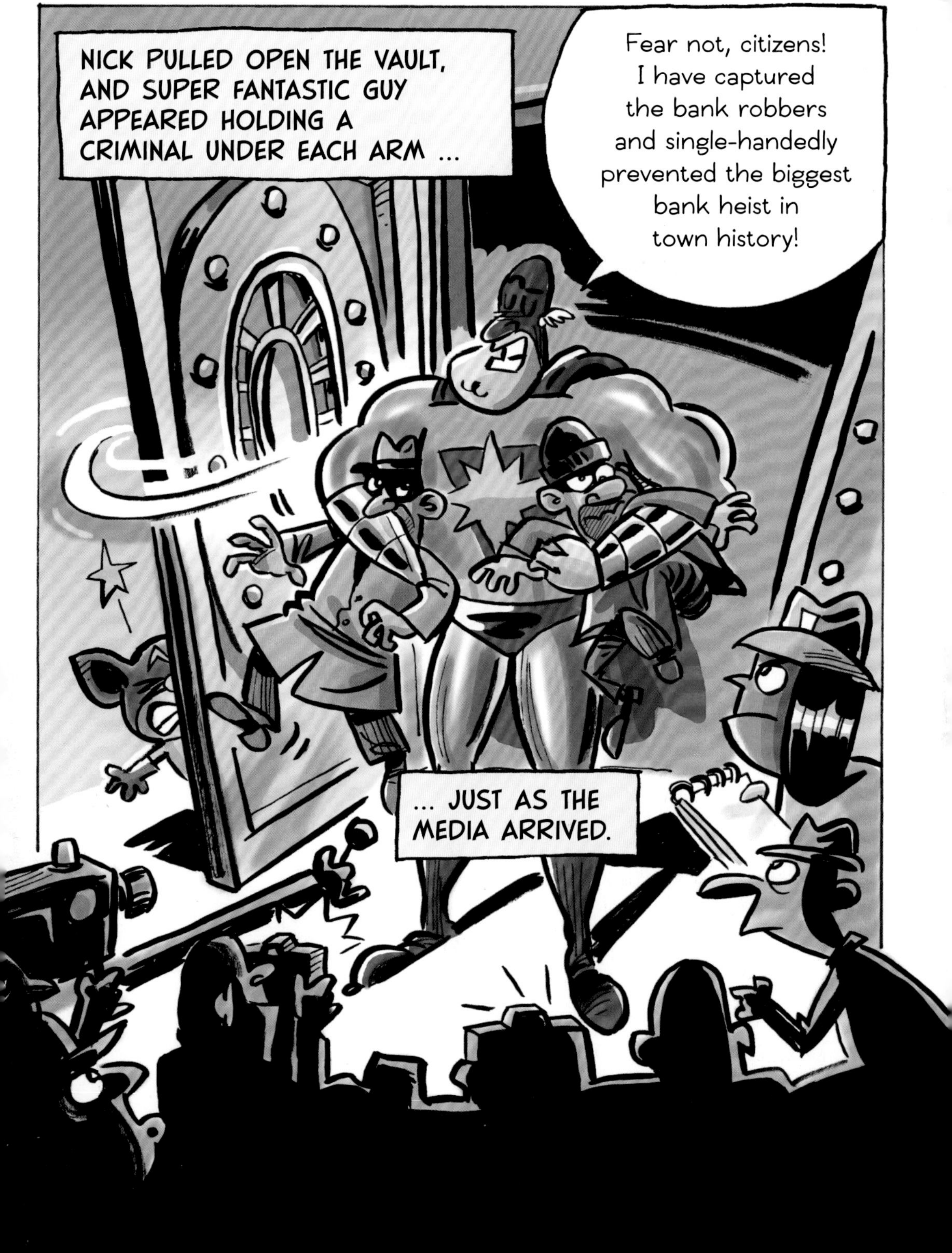
NICK PULLED OPEN THE VAULT, AND SUPER FANTASTIC GUY APPEARED HOLDING A CRIMINAL UNDER EACH ARM ...
Fear not, citizens! I have captured the bank robbers and single-handedly prevented the biggest bank heist in town history!
... JUST AS THE MEDIA ARRIVED.

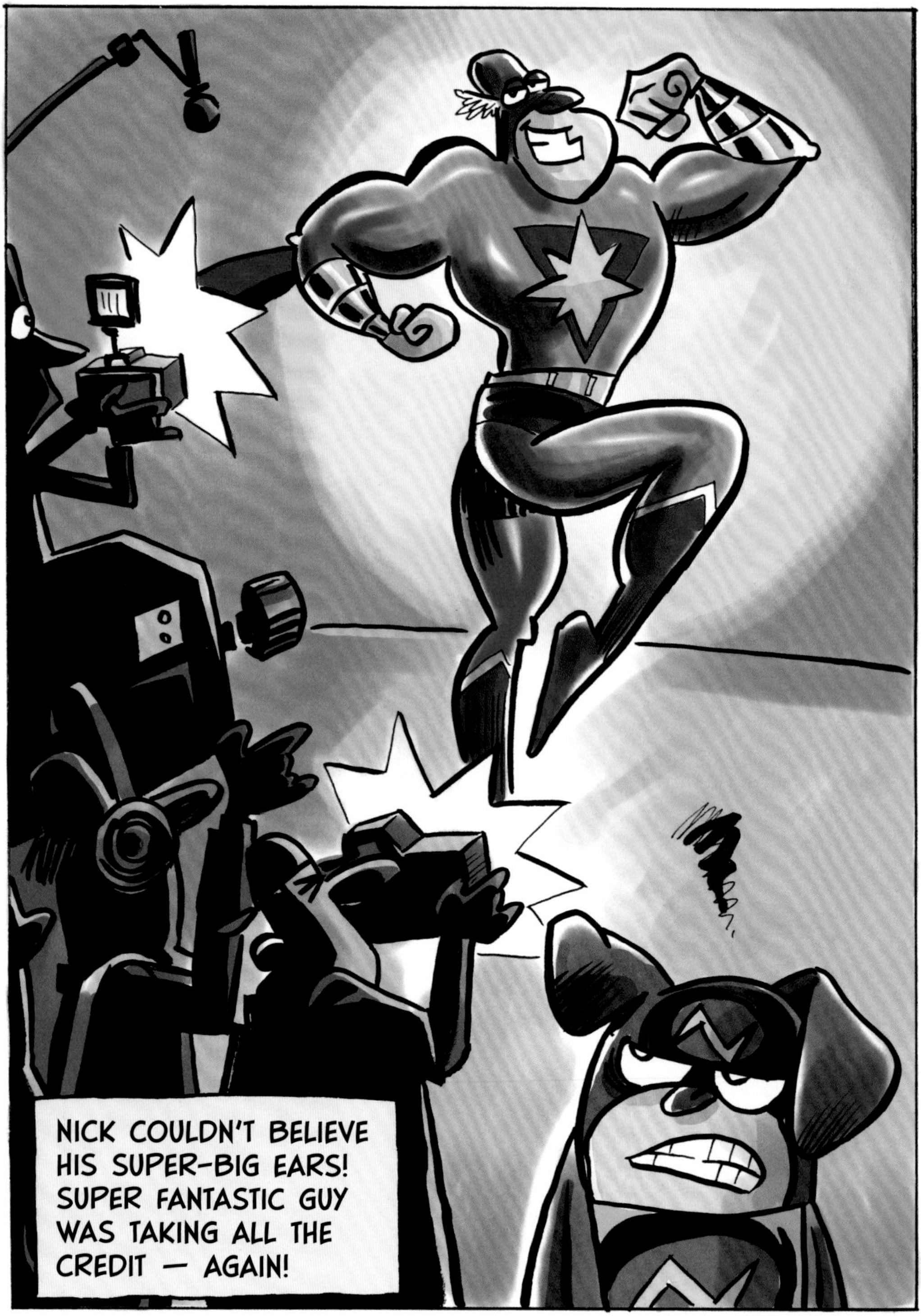
NICK COULDN'T BELIEVE HIS SUPER-BIG EARS! SUPER FANTASTIC GUY WAS TAKING ALL THE CREDIT — AGAIN!

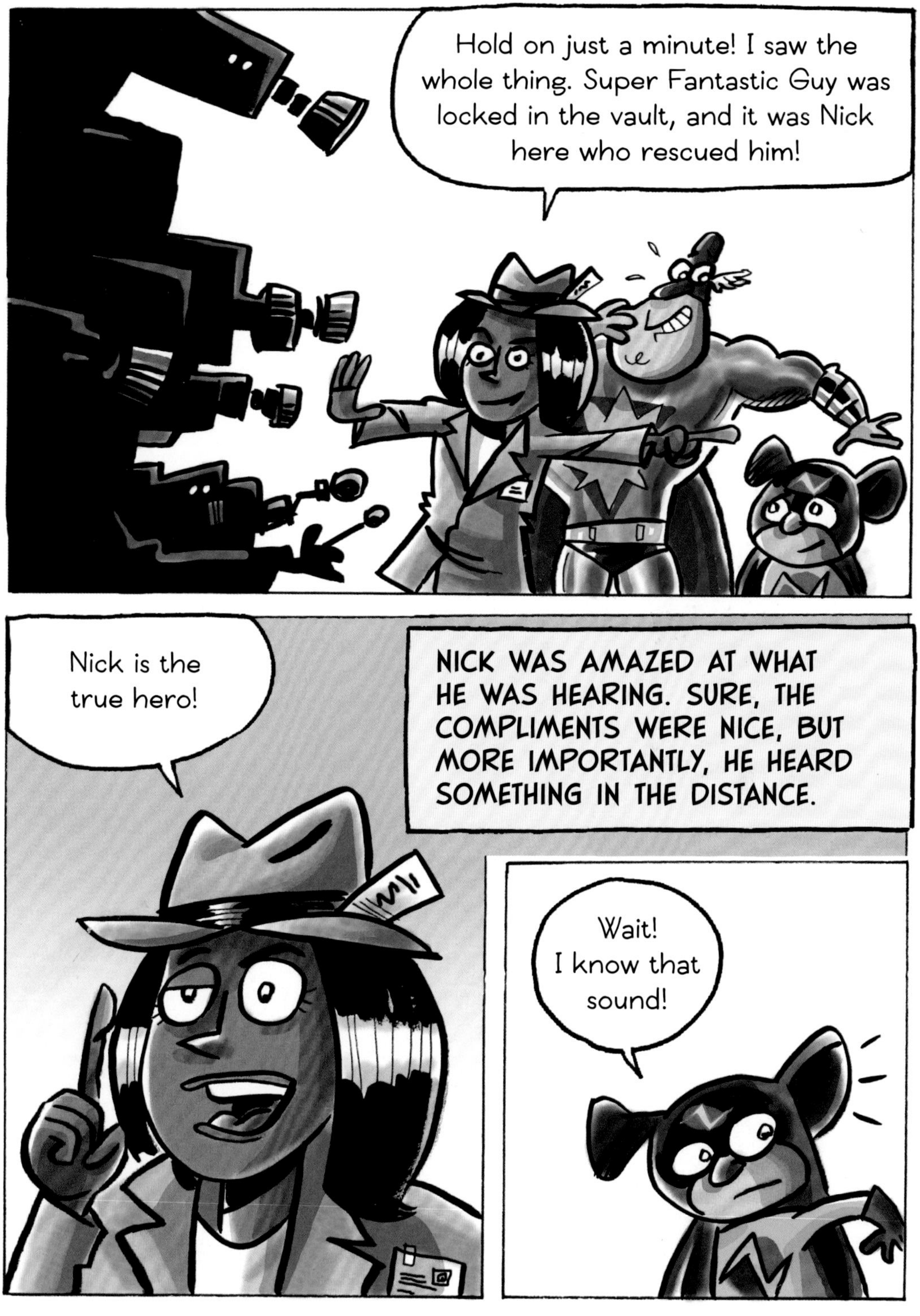

Hold on just a minute! I saw the whole thing. Super Fantastic Guy was locked in the vault, and it was Nick here who rescued him!
Nick is the true hero!
NICK WAS AMAZED AT WHAT HE WAS HEARING. SURE, THE COMPLIMENTS WERE NICE, BUT MORE IMPORTANTLY, HE HEARD SOMETHING IN THE DISTANCE.
Wait! I know that sound!

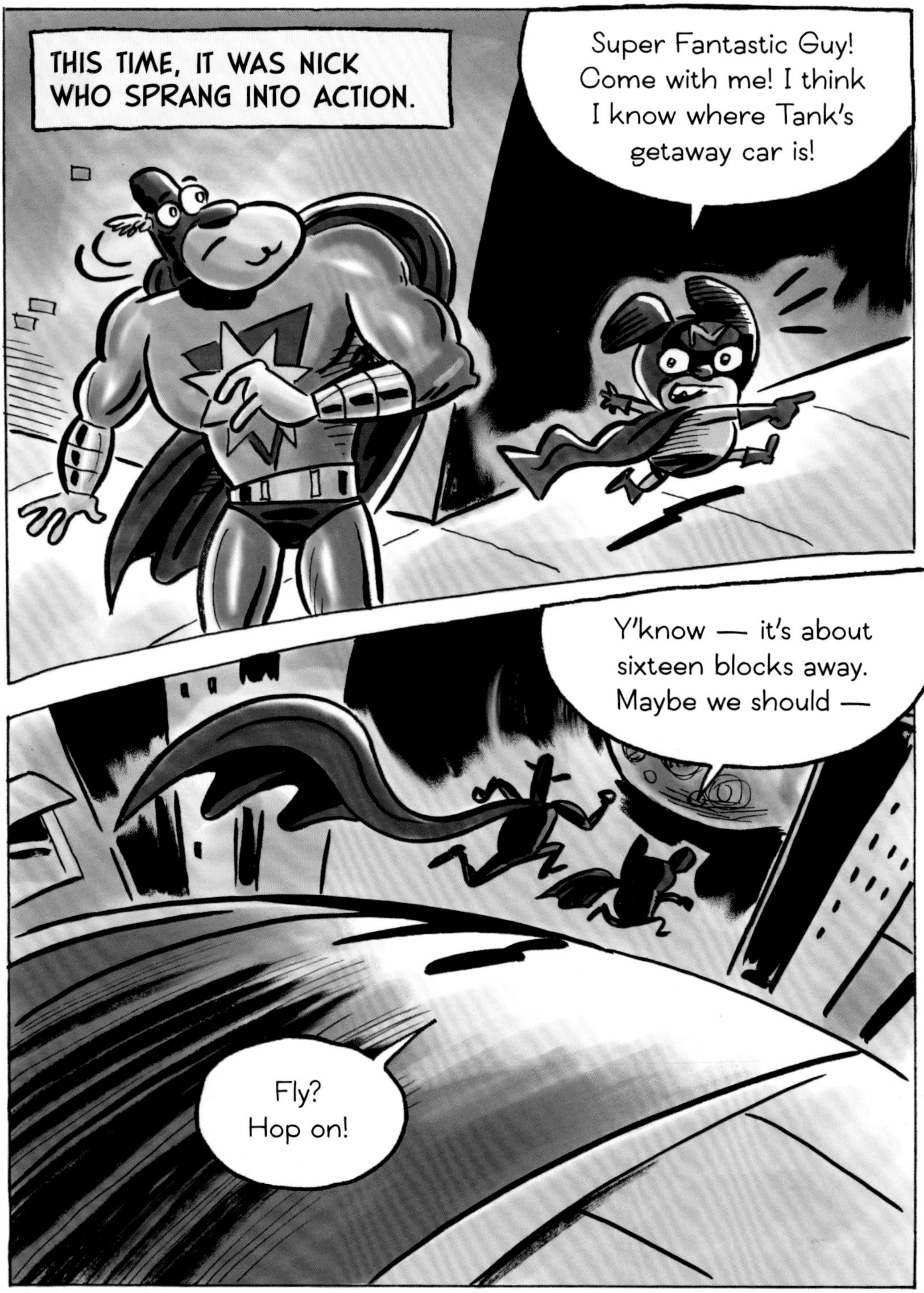
THIS TIME, IT WAS NICK WHO SPRANG INTO ACTION.
Super Fantastic Guy! Come with me! I think I know where Tank's getaway car is!
Y'know — it's about sixteen blocks away. Maybe we should —
Fly? Hop on!

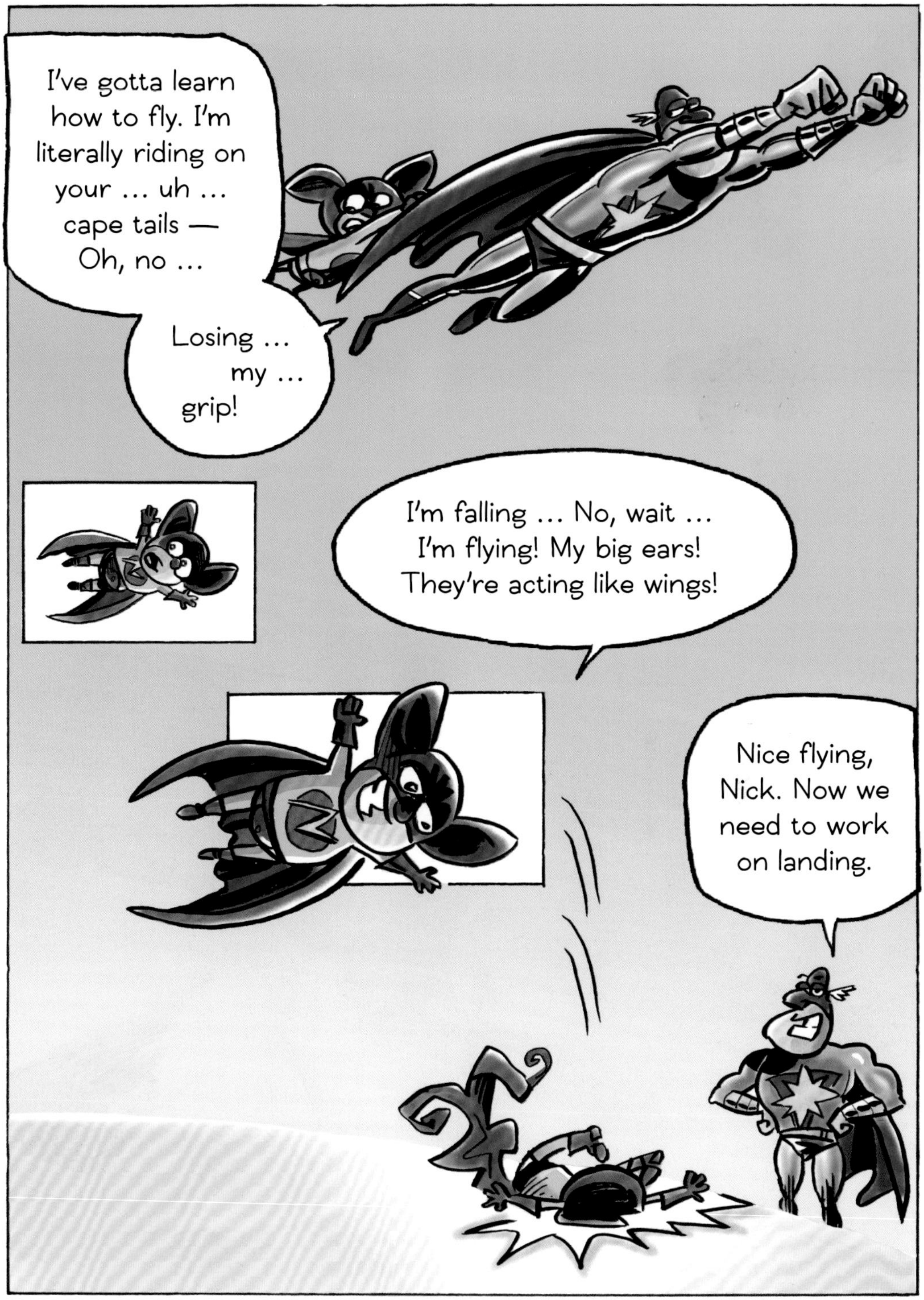
I've gotta learn how to fly. I'm literally riding on your ... uh ... cape tails — Oh, no ...
Losing ... my ... grip!
I'm falling ... No, wait ... I'm flying! My big ears! They're acting like wings!
Nice flying, Nick. Now we need to work on landing.

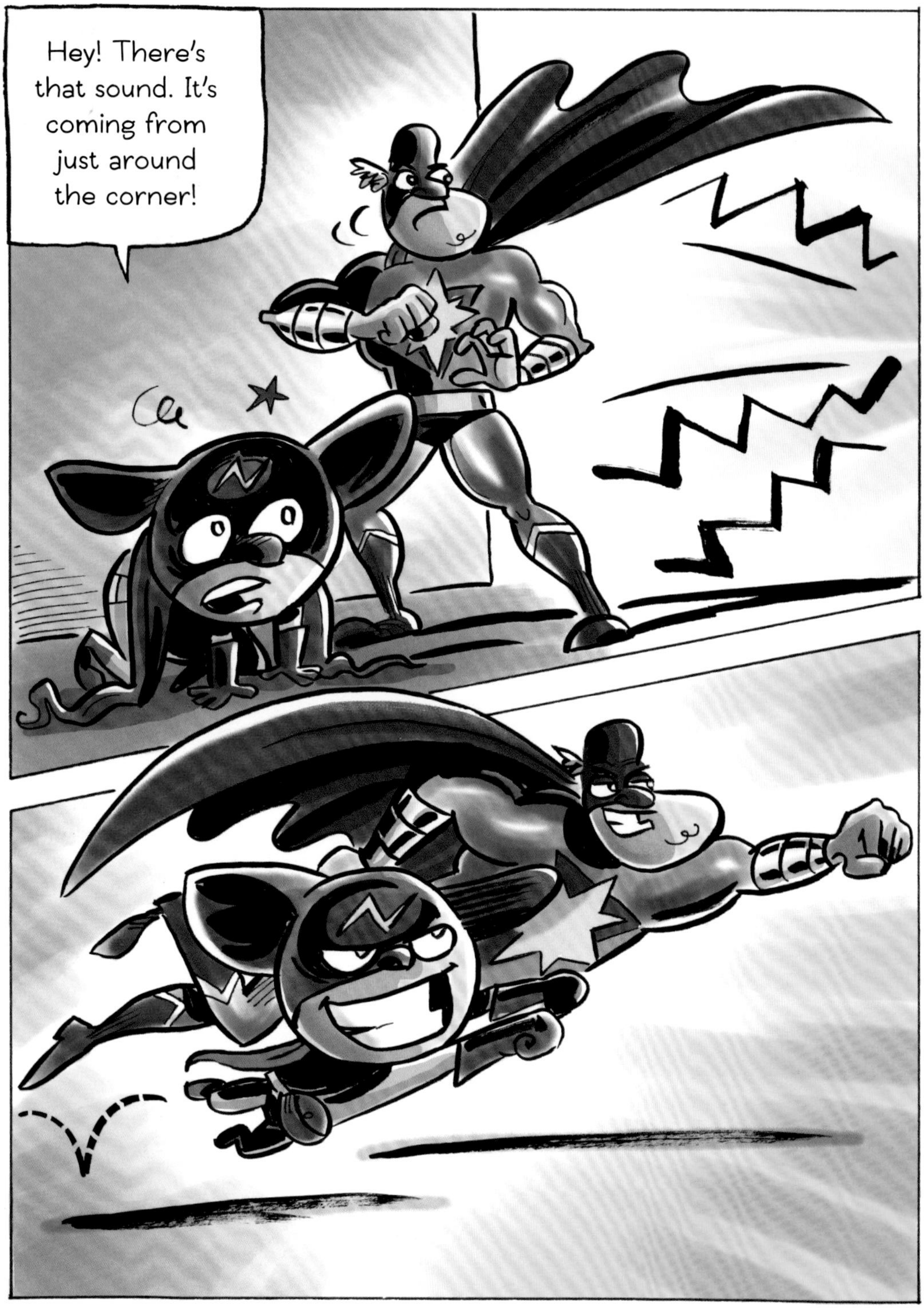
Hey! There's that sound. It's coming from just around the corner!

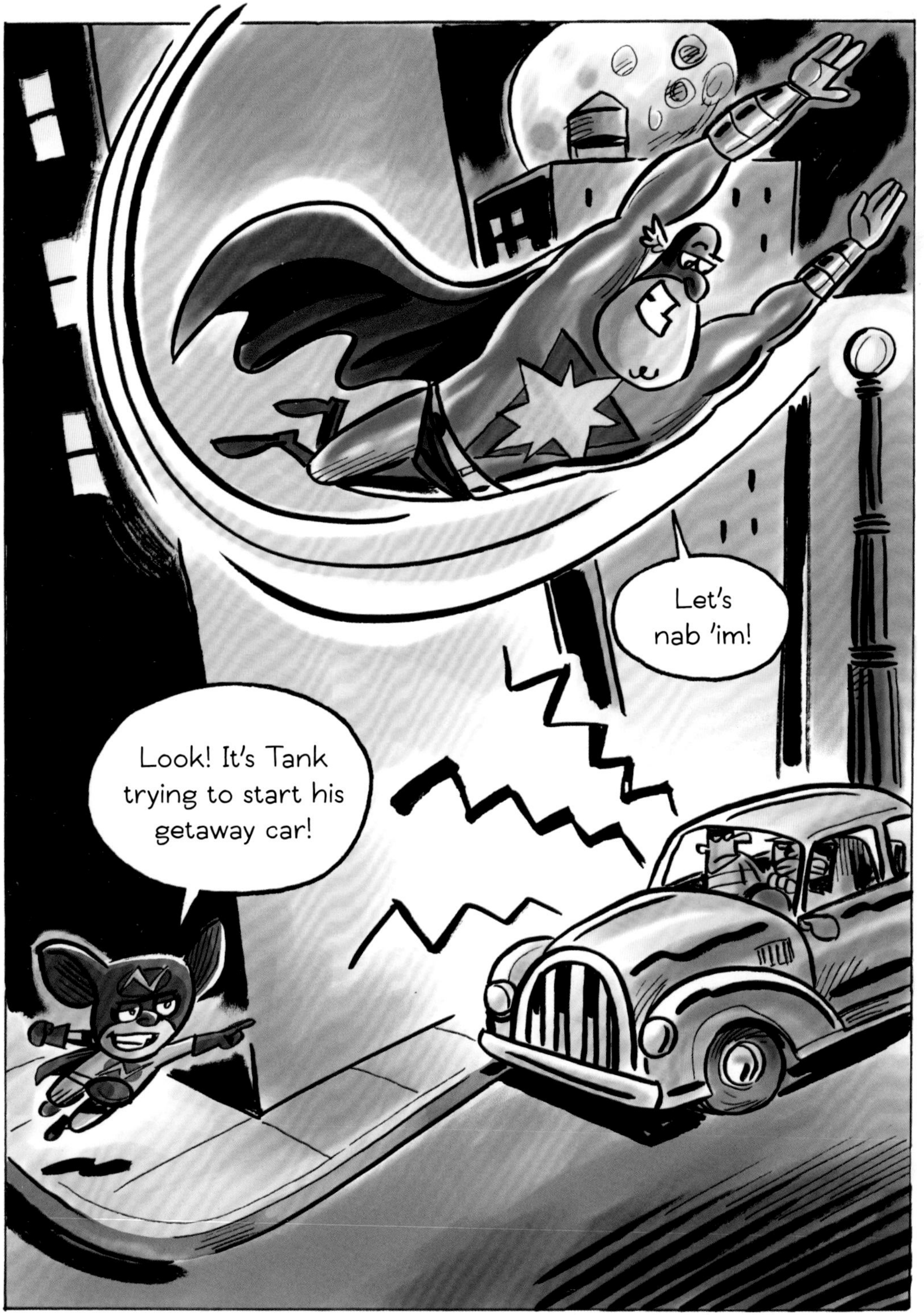
Look! It's Tank trying to start his getaway car!
Let's nab 'im!

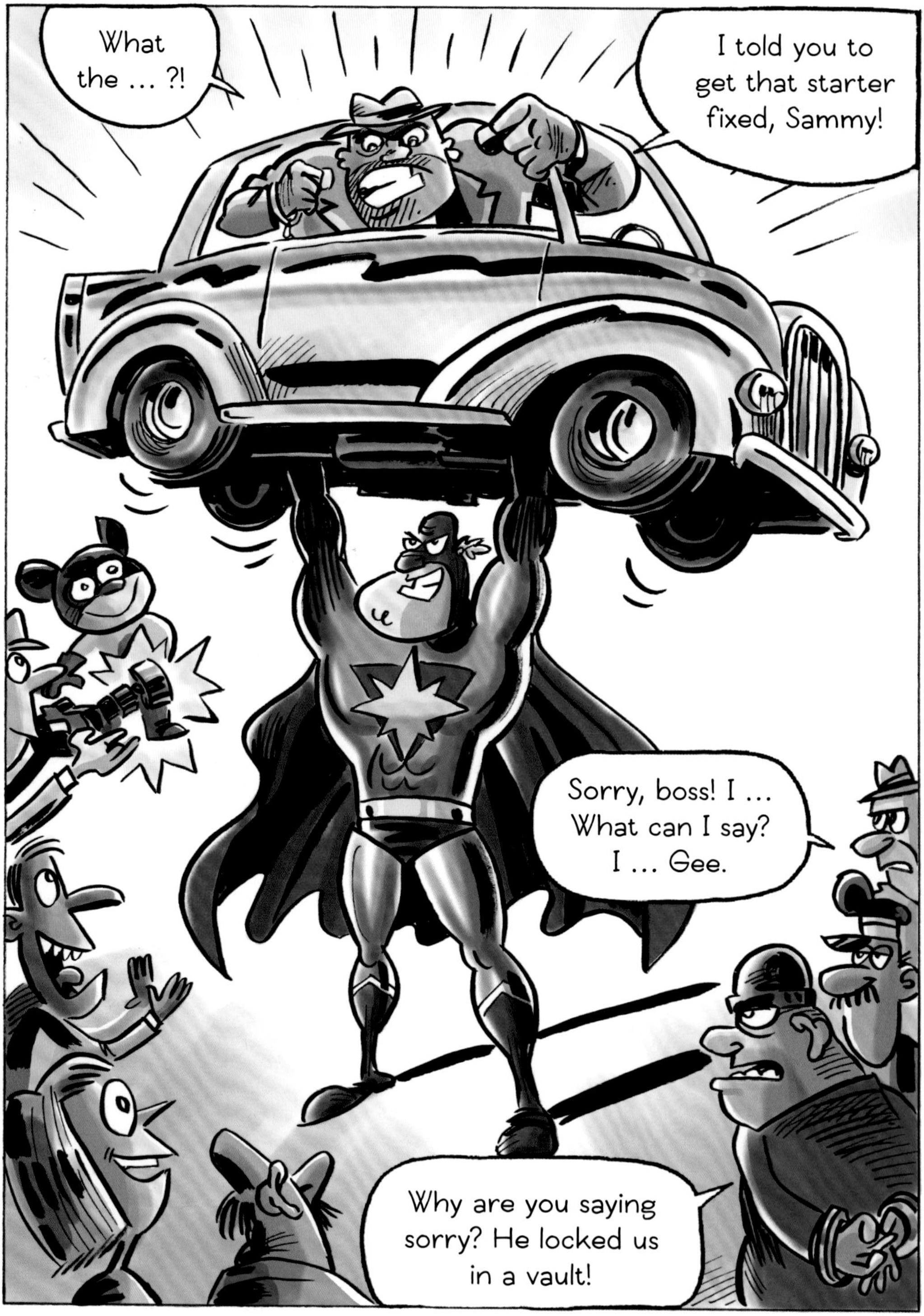
What the ... ?!
I told you to get that starter fixed, Sammy!
Sorry, boss! I ... What can I say? I ... Gee.
Why are you saying sorry? He locked us in a vault!

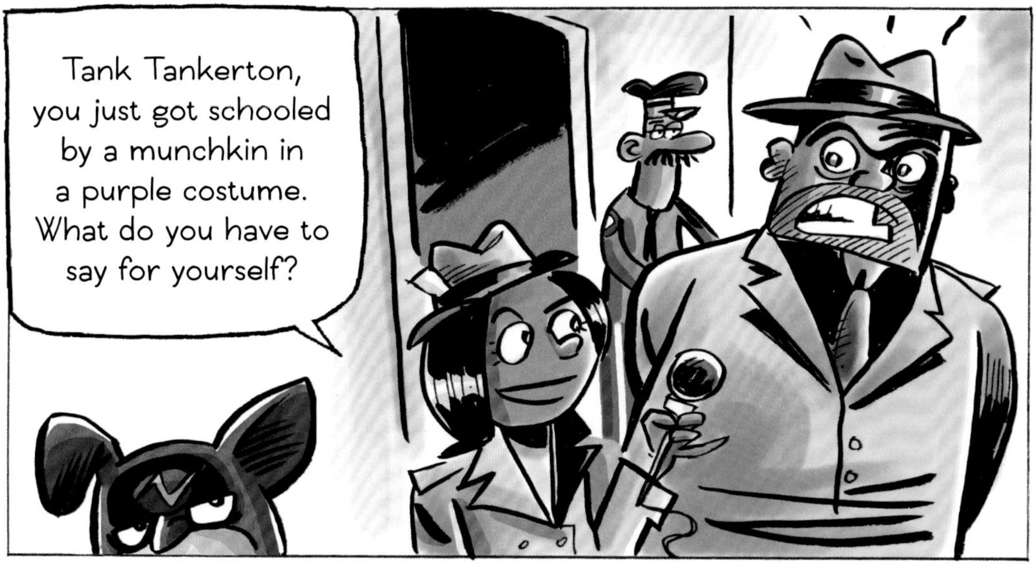
Tank Tankerton, you just got schooled by a munchkin in a purple costume. What do you have to say for yourself?

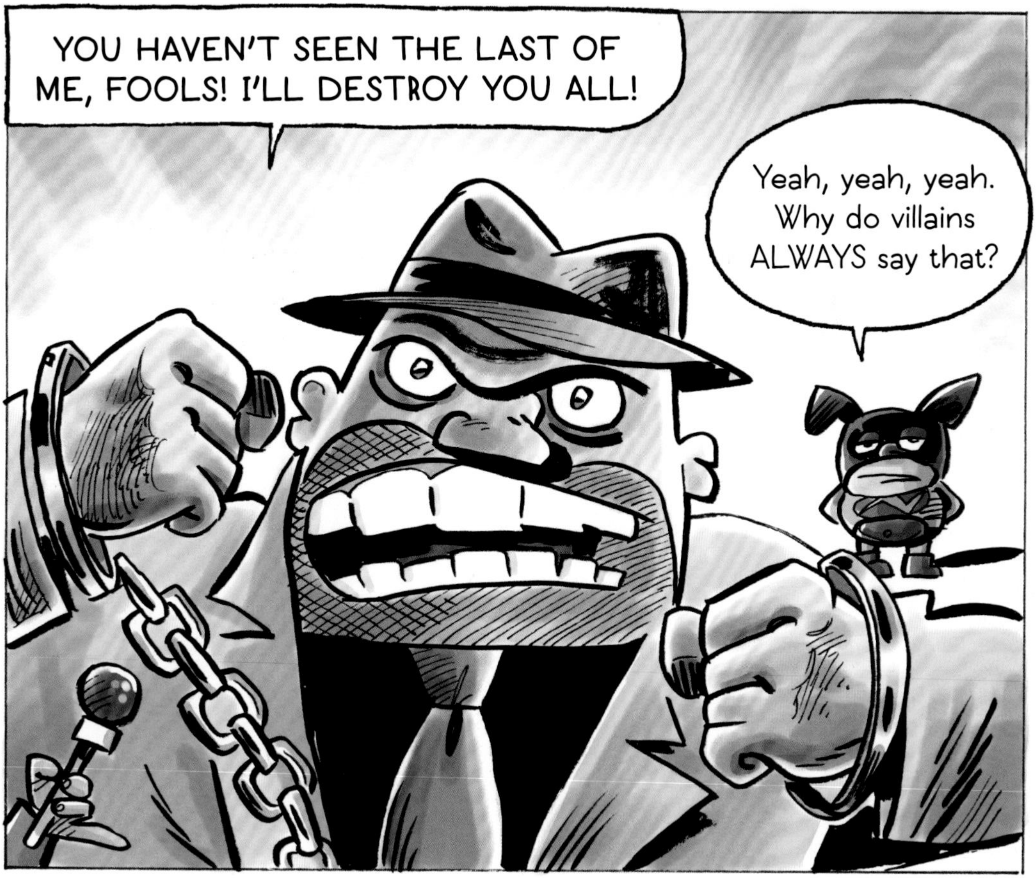
YOU HAVEN'T SEEN THE LAST OF ME, FOOLS! I'LL DESTROY YOU ALL!
Yeah, yeah, yeah. Why do villains ALWAYS say that?

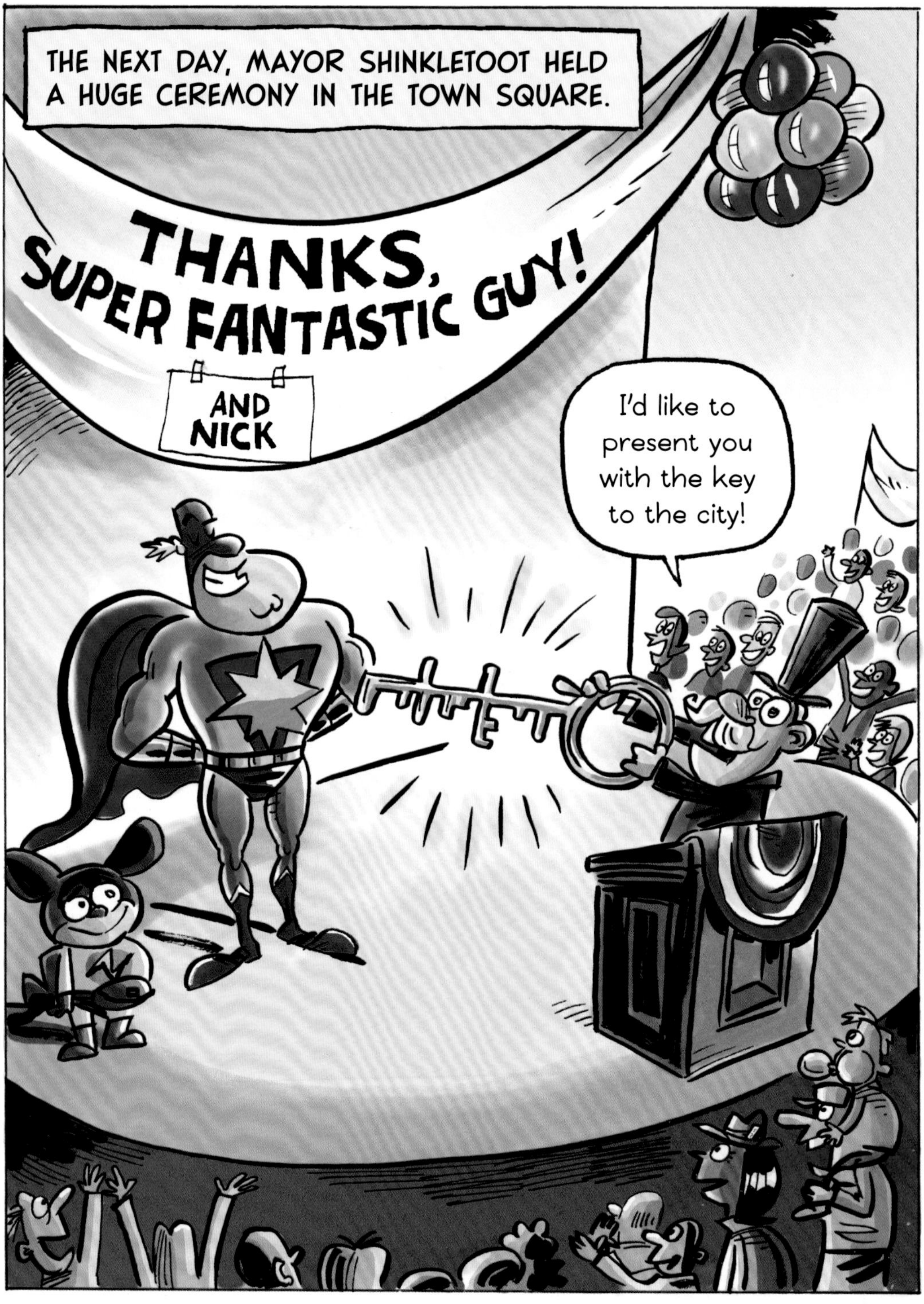
THE NEXT DAY, MAYOR SHINKLETOOT HELD A HUGE CEREMONY IN THE TOWN SQUARE.
THANKS, SUPER FANTASTIC GUY!
AND NICK
I'd like to present you with the key to the city!

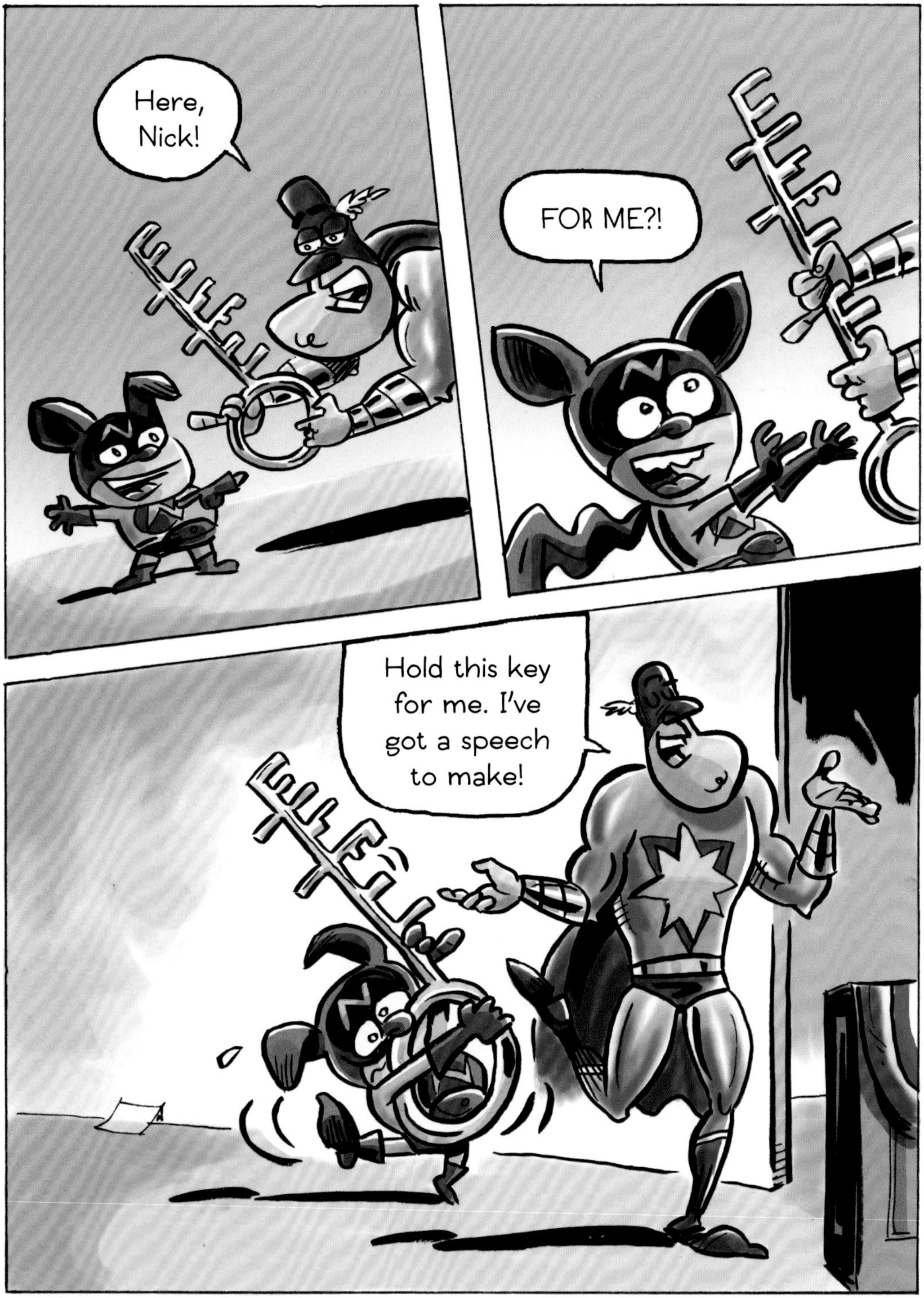
Here, Nick!
FOR ME?!
Hold this key for me. I've got a speech to make!

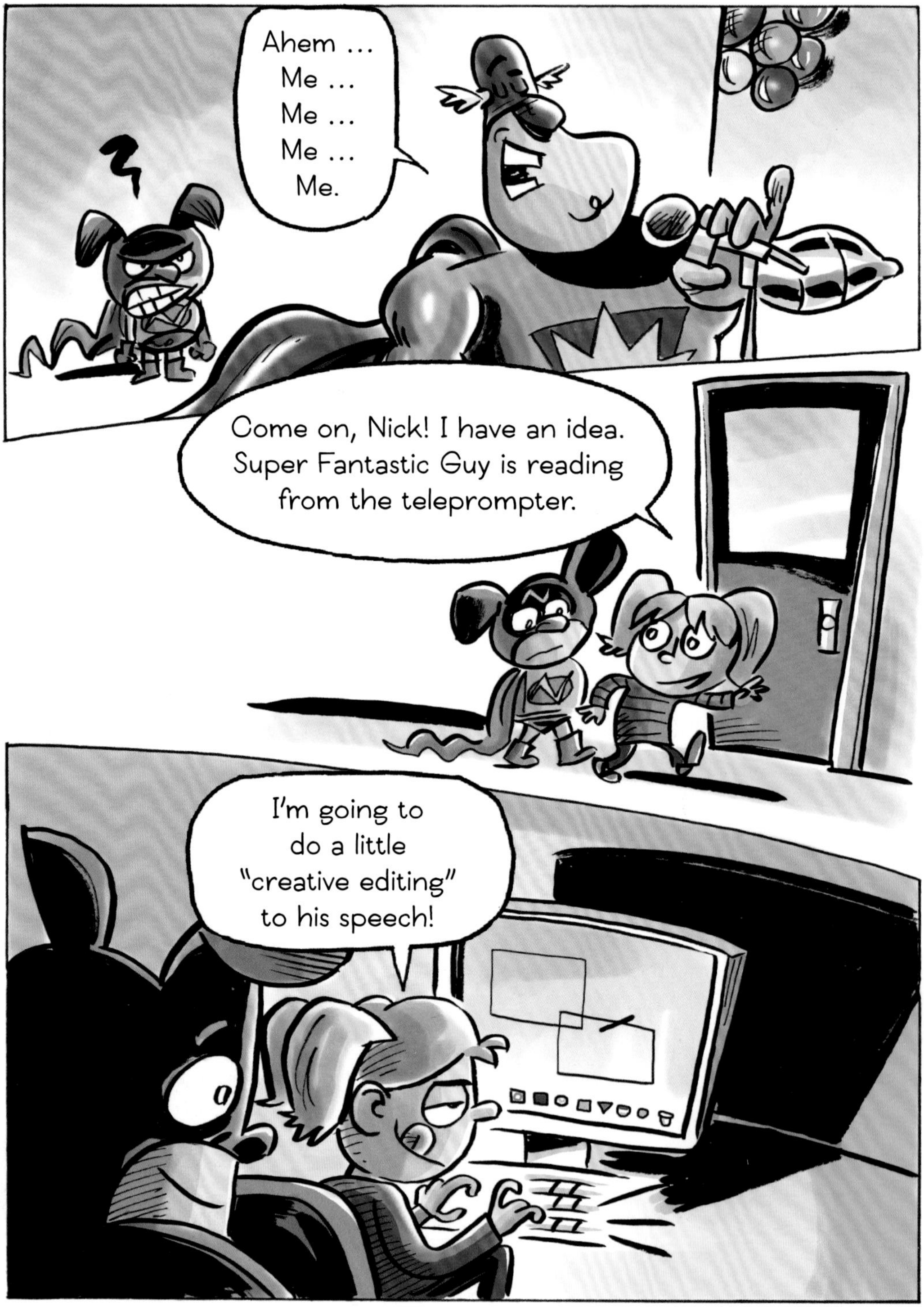
Ahem ... Me ... Me ... Me ... Me.
Come on, Nick! I have an idea. Super Fantastic Guy is reading from the teleprompter.
I'm going to do a little "creative editing" to his speech!

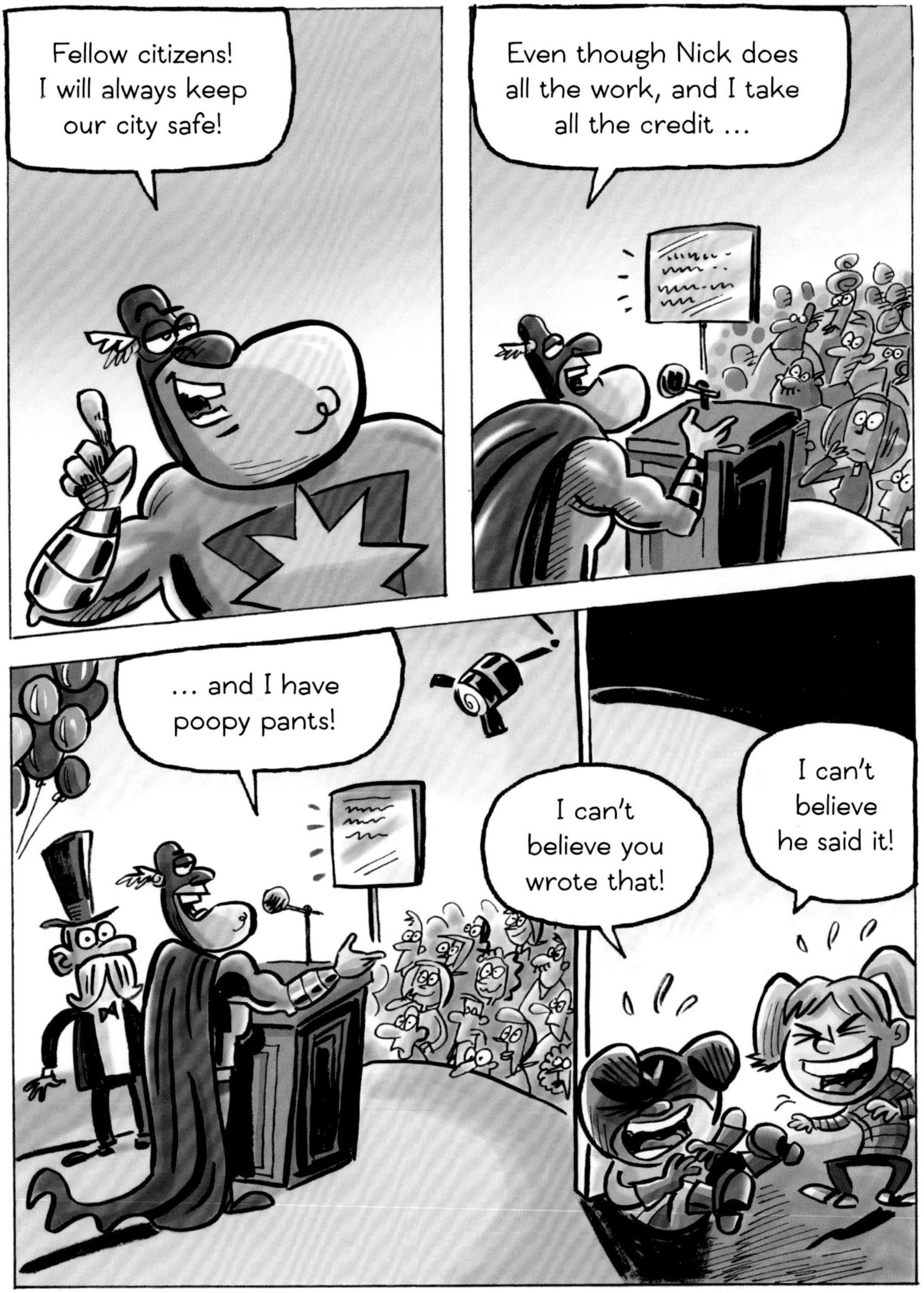
Fellow citizens! I will always keep our city safe!
Even though Nick does all the work, and I take all the credit ...
... and I have poopy pants!
I can't believe you wrote that!
I can't believe he said it!

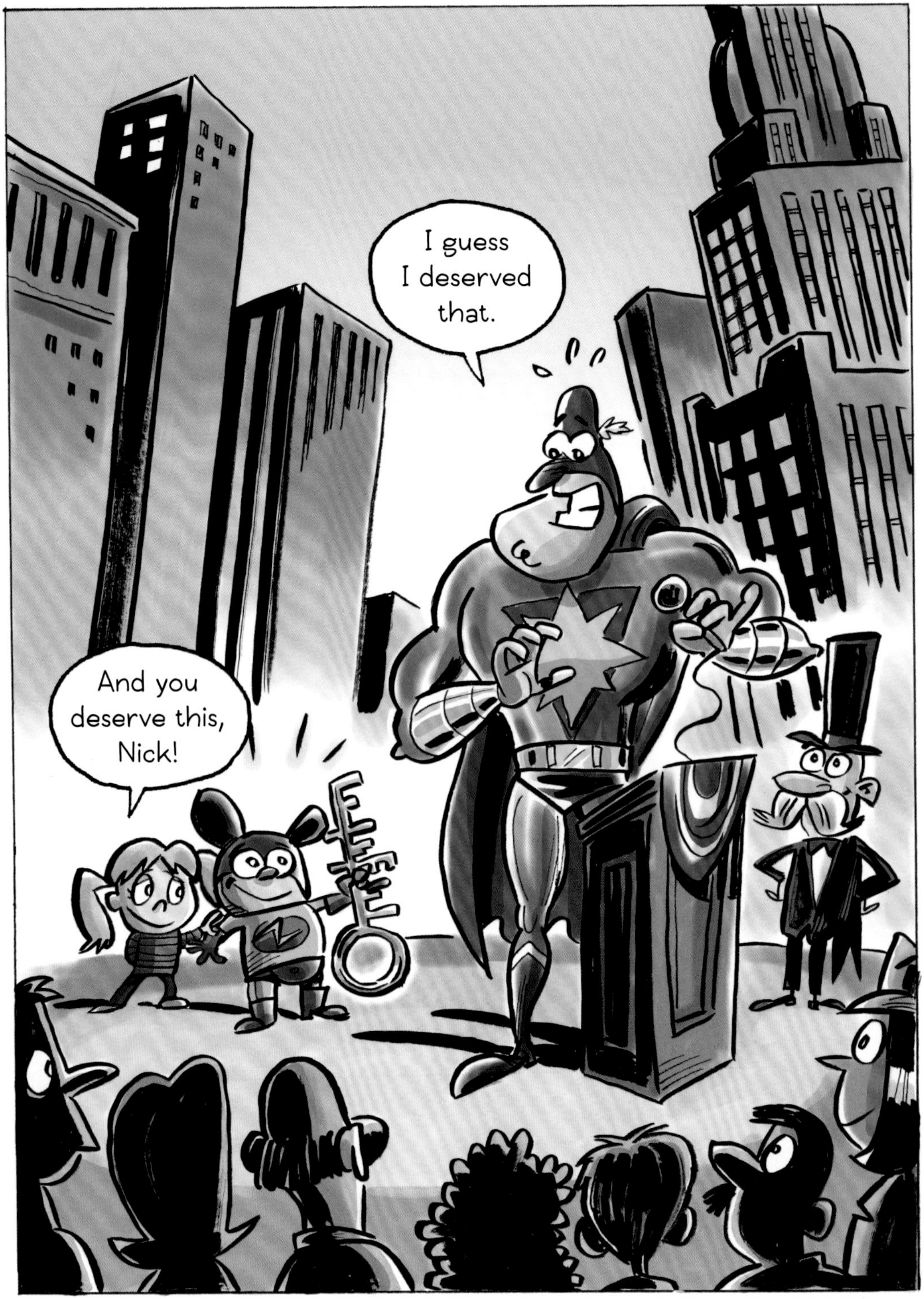
I guess I deserved that.
And you deserve this, Nick!